Gareth Clarke

WHAT IS IS

HZPublishing

Copyright © 2025 by Gareth Clarke

All rights reserved. No part of this book may be reproduced or used in any manner without written permission of the copyright owner except for the use of quotations in a book review. For more information, address: garethclarke137@gmail.com

HZPublishing

What Is Is

CONTENTS

Mr No-win	9
Fear of God	11
Booking in Advance	23
Difficulty in Crossing a Road	27
The Fly	30
The Secret	32
The Hall	34
Flamboyant Eternity	36
Harrogate 3440	38
Creaking Jesus	41
The Project	44
Androphobia	58
A Sunny Morning	65
The Loneliness of Traffic Lights	67
Chemical Romance	68
Two's Company	70
A Matter of Supreme Importance	73
The Interrogation	78

Too Tough	81
A Complete Mystery	82
You Expect Me to be Warm in Manner	85
The Time Traveller	88
My So-called Life	92
The Doll	93
The Little Fleckers	95
Which Slice of Bread	110
Every Last Stone or Pebble	112
Why Do You Appear to be Inert?	113
Nales Place	116
The Music Teacher	118
The World Awoke	122
Betrayed by Myself	127
The Unopened Parcels	128
Getting There	129
My Little One	130
Chance Encounter	133
Fwuck	135
The Plague of Beards	136

Everything Simply Evaporates	158
The Poet	159
Making a Difference	161
The Power Station	165
Buck	167
The Unanswered Questions	172
The Old Man	175
Miriam	176
The Search for Meaning	181
To My Daughter	183
The Lodge House	193
Perfidy	196
Then We'll Be Done	199
Jackwagon Blues	208
The Melancholy of the Hour	210
What Is Is	212

appear from nowhere (more likely the depths of the bin) and proceeded to make a beeline for my face. A few minutes later my hated neighbour started up with the usual loud, thumping music. Quarter of an hour passed, by which time I had a raging headache. Thought of banging on the wall, didn't. My nose now completely blocked. Can hardly breathe. Yet another cold. Just get clear of one, and another one comes along.

And so it continues, or continued (can't decide on the tense) - the buses missed by thirty seconds, the unanswered texts, the cold looks, false accusations, mistakes, missteps, self-abuse, self-loathing, and so on - until eventually it's time for bed once more. Couldn't get to sleep again. Another long, uncomfortable night. And so on.

Fear of God

'This is my letter of resignation.'

The Bishop frowned, took an ivory-handled knife from his desk and ripped the envelope open.

I had no idea how to resign as a Church of England vicar. I didn't even know if there were any precedents. I supposed there must be, but I'd never heard or read of it happening.

Time seemed to stand still. The Bishop was a tall, robust man of later middle age with a powerful, almost intimidating presence, looking very much like James Robertson Justice in a cassock, and with the same elegantly sculpted and pointed beard. Perhaps he had modelled himself on the actor. Perhaps it was *all* an act, and this was a stage set, and I was only pretending to abruptly terminate what I had thought of all my life as my vocation.

Suddenly, having read my resignation note and thrown it down on his desk, he laughed heartily.

'You've lost your faith because of what is written in the Bible?'

'Well, that's part of it.'

'My dear Horace, you shouldn't take it all so literally! The Bible is just a rag-bag of stories and fables scribbled down over a very long period by more or less backward and ignorant people in archaic times, all with differing agendas, and all of it written when pretty much everyone knew less than nothing. That's not to say that many of the stories aren't highly imaginative and entertaining, of course they are. And also that they provide a window into the society and thinking, the belief systems and superstitions of those who wrote them. But they have no direct relevance to us in the modern age - beyond, of course, the historical fact of having played a role in shaping many of the accepted norms and values of current society. But fundamentally they are simply fables, fairy tales, fictions. Nothing more.'

'I thought the Bible was supposed to be the Word of God.'

'My dear boy!'

'Then what are we doing here? What are *you* doing here? Why did you take the cloth?'

'Faith, Horace! Faith! Faith that God exists. Faith that God is good.'

'That's precisely the trouble. I've lost my faith. And I no longer believe that God is good.'

'Because of what is written in the Bible? Ridiculous! In any case - so you've lost your faith. Happens to all of us from time to time. You'll get it back. Purely temporary. You'll see.'

'No, it's not exactly that. I'm not explaining myself very well. I suppose I haven't lost my faith as such.'

'Then what?'

'It's what you said. You believe that God is good. I no longer do. I believe that, if God does exist, He is evil beyond measure.' The Bishop was now regarding me with an ambivalent expression, half serious, half amused. 'And that if we believe in anything, we should implore that thing, whatever it may be, on our hands and knees, that He does not exist.'

The Bishop went over to a small table on which there were several bottles, selected one, then poured out two generous glassfuls.

'Here, drink this. Medicinal. Do you good.'

I took the proffered glass, though I rarely drink beyond the occasional small glass of sherry prior to dinner. The brandy imparted a warm, comforting glow in the pit of my stomach. I am not a natural speaker, but the drink seemed to have the gradual effect of loosening my tongue.

'You're not making a great deal of sense, Horace. You say that God is evil. Where's your evidence?'

'It's everywhere. It's everywhere you look. It's right before us every single day in the blood-soaked horror of existence. And it's certainly evident throughout the Bible. The Biblical God is a jealous, insecure, boastful, capricious, sadistic, murderous - '

'As I said before, don't take everything in the Bible seriously.'

I went on, barely aware of the Bishop's interjection.

'All this quite apart from man's barbarism towards his fellow man through the ages, and quite apart from the absolute horror of the natural world - the "red in tooth and claw" reality of nature, with no sight or sound or glimpse to be found anywhere of anything resembling divine mercy. As far as my own faith goes, that is faith in the existence of God, all I really know is that I don't know - that is, I'm not sure. But I now believe that if God does exist, it would be an incomparably worse situation than if He doesn't. It would be infinitely dangerous, in fact horrific. Heaven would effectively be Hell. It would be the equivalent of incarceration, not just for a specified length of time, or even for a lifetime, but for an infinity - and all at the mercy of a lunatic jailer, with no right of appeal. It's a nightmarish prospect beyond most people's imagination. I'm become not merely afraid, but frankly terrified at the very idea of God. The concept of an all-powerful God fills me with abject fear.'

There was a long silence.

'You still haven't provided me with any evidence to substantiate this claim that God is evil.'

'You're a scholar, you know far more about the Bible than I. To quote the Bible to you - '

'Heavens, man, forget all that!' He was now striding about the study jabbing ferociously at imagined enemies with his pipe. 'Have the courage of your convictions.'

'Very well.'

'In fact,' suddenly turning and thrusting the pipe at me, 'answer me this. Why did you become a priest in the first place?'

I considered this question for perhaps the best part of a minute. Meanwhile the Bishop retired behind his desk and forbore to interrupt my meditations, and was soon puffing away on his pipe, filling the study with fragrant grey smoke like incense, as if to erect a barrier between himself and my heresies.

I told him that primarily I had been drawn to the pastoral aspects of a priest's work, and that my faith had sprung from the notion of doing God's work in providing comfort and succour to people in distress, or those in need of spiritual guidance or support. Instead of my faith driving my desire to be a priest, I believed that the desire to be part of a community and to do "good works" had come first, and my faith, such as it was, and which I had never examined very closely, but had more or less taken for granted, had followed on and grown with time. Until, that is, I had become beset and now almost overwhelmed by doubts.

The Bishop took in this explanation without comment, then repeated his request that I provide evidence of God's evil nature.

And so, beginning with Genesis and the Flood - "And the LORD said, I will destroy man whom I have created from the face of the earth; both man, and beast, and the creeping thing, and the fowls of the air; for it repenteth me that I have made them." On through an eye for an eye, and visiting the sins of the fathers upon the children, and upon the children's children. And on through Leviticus and Numbers - "shall surely be put to death", and "I will smite them with pestilence", and on and on through the endless threats and yet more threats, of stoning and of wholesale destruction, of endorsement of slavery, of demands for revenge, of mass murder and famine, of subjection, lies and deceit, and calls for mass rape, and of laws founded on the vilest misogyny. And on through the rabid vindictiveness of His curses for disobeying or failing to observe all of His commandments and statutes. "For the LORD, whose name is Jealous, is a jealous God." Quoting book after book, chapter and verse, so far as I could remember them. On through Deuteronomy and Samuel and Kings and Job and Isaiah, and Jeremiah and Hosea and Zechariah. Verses in Deuteronomy for some reason etched on my mind - "The LORD will smite thee with the botch of Egypt, and with the emerods, and with the scab, and with the itch, whereof thou canst not be healed. The LORD shall smite thee with madness, and blindness, and astonishment of heart: And thou shalt grope at noonday, as the blind gropeth in darkness, and thou shalt not prosper in thy ways: and thou shalt be only oppressed and spoiled evermore, and no man shall save thee." And "See now that I, *even* I, *am* he, and *there is* no god with me: I kill, and I make alive; I wound, and I heal: neither *is there any* that can deliver out of my hand." And "I will make mine arrows drunk with blood, and my sword shall devour flesh; *and that* with the blood of the slain and of the captives, from the beginning of revenges upon the enemy." And on through all the injunctions to slay and utterly destroy and slaughter children - "their infants shall be dashed in pieces, and their women with child shall be ripped up."

'It's all slaughter and slaughter and slaughter upon meaningless slaughter,' in a voice of high emotion to the now near-invisible entity wreathed in smoke (as if about to self-immolate in protest at my flagrant apostasies). Carried away (the brandy having now comprehensively loosened my inhibitions and my tongue) into unaccustomed flights of oratory. "' I form the light, and create darkness: I make peace, and create evil: I the LORD do all these things."

'I entirely agree with you, that the Bible *is* a vile, ridiculous, archaic book, full of arbitrary cruelties. It's a handbook for violence and lunacy and retribution and jealousy, and insecurity and unchallenged patriarchy and misogyny. It is everything that is despicable and evil. And our so-called God is clearly not merely despicable and evil, but also desperately insecure, striking out in all directions in His insecurity and a pathological need to dominate.'

I could hardly make out the Bishop at all by this time, cloaked behind his screen of tobacco smoke. But as I finished, the cloud gradually rolled away to reveal his imposing, even forbidding figure now standing behind the desk. He strode towards me, and I felt a sudden unaccountable deep fear. But in fact he merely took my glass and proceeded to refill it, this time with a splash of soda, for - as he put it - I was looking a little hot and bothered.

I had been standing while delivering my lengthy speech, of which I now felt more than a little embarrassed. The Bishop, however, betrayed no anger or indignation, but motioned me to a leather armchair, and sank down himself in the one opposite. I was glad to sit down; I felt exhausted, quite spent.

Without responding directly to what I had said, he began to speak, quietly but with firm assurance, his eyes fixed on mine, proposing various fantastical theories, scarcely believable, and certainly contrary to the accepted teachings of the modern Church. In the confusion of my feelings at that moment I don't remember much of what he said - a lot of it was frankly horrific, or else highly esoteric, relating to reincarnation, telepathy, second sight, extraterrestrial beings - sky people, the Anunnaki - demons, demonic possession, blood sacrifices, torture. I struggled to see how any of this related to my doubts about God's good intentions.

But then he began talking of Jesus and Yahweh and Theos, the Creator, and the Father, the One in the Skies, the One in the Heavens, and Marcion of Sinope, and the Gnostics of the early Christian Church.

'Strenuous efforts were made by Marcion and the Gnostics to draw a line between the Hebrew God, Yahweh, the God of the Old Testament - the violent warrior king, just as you have portrayed him - and the loving, merciful God of Jesus. They thought that these entities were incompatible. They claimed that Yahweh wasn't God at all, that he was instead the Demiurge, the Craftsman, the Creator of the physical world over which He could rule, a lesser God antithetical to the Supreme Being who existed on a higher, purely spiritual plane. They believed that a Divine Spark, a fragment of the true God, exists within everyone. And they called it the Light, the eternal, spiritual part of our being that Yahweh can't control.'

And on and on he went, on how the Egyptians had contrived a powerful myth to counter the scandal and humiliation of the Exodus, portraying Yahweh as a donkey-headed demon, linking the demonic Set of the Egyptian pantheon, God of storms, violence and chaos, together with the Canaanite storm God Baal, with an entity which Marcion argued wasn't a God at all, but instead a malevolent Creator, murdering and enslaving. An horrific, jealous, rage-filled being. And so Yahweh had become this demonical figure, with the Cosmos as a spiritual prison with the human soul trapped within a physical body, desperate only to escape the nightmare of corporeal existence. And to counter this, to set against all the madness and mayhem, there would appear the executed carpenter of Nazareth, Jesus, who became the Divine Christ, the Holy Redeemer, the Son of God!

At last he stopped speaking, and in the silence that followed refilled and lit his pipe with quiet deliberation, before once more looking directly into my eyes. I struggled to meet his gaze.

'But of course there is no Divine Spark, Horace, no Light, no fragment of the Divine Spirit. There is nothing within us that is remotely divine.'

And at these words he grinned widely, uncannily, as if at some in-joke, his face and whole demeanour suddenly completely unlike himself.

'In fact all of those doctrines and theories and myths from centuries ago are nothing more than absolute nonsense! Fantastical inventions! Fictions! You see,

Horace, there is in fact only one entity that we might call God, only one Creator, one Spirit. Give Him whatever name you like, be it God, Yahweh, Satan, Set, Demiurge, Allah, Jehovah, Lucifer, Creator, Holy Spirit, Baal, Beelzebub, Ruler of Darkness, Jailer, Deceiver. They are all one and the same! He is *all things*! He is *Everything*! These alternate names are merely figures of speech. It, He, they, are not separate, autonomous entities, and they never were. God is as surely Satan as He is Yahweh as he is the Demiurge, and so on! God is God, the only God. *And* He is the Devil, *and* He is everything else! For God is quite literally Everything!

I was now sweating and shaking in my chair. The study within the Bishop's Palace had become my prison cell and I was the hapless prisoner, and the Bishop was my jailer.

'Do you believe in the supernatural, Horace?' he asked casually. 'Ghosts, demons, spirits and the like?'

I stammered something to the effect that I hadn't had any first-hand experience.

'Oh it's all true. It's all quite true.'

To my horror there was something overtly malevolent now in his expression. And even his voice, when he spoke, had a malignant tone.

'Demons are real, Horace, and they are everywhere. Non-corporeal in themselves, they often take human form, or inhabit a human vessel, where the humanity within has been completely displaced.'

At this moment his eyes, coal-black, which I had not really noticed before, seemed momentarily to flicker, and the room went suddenly very cold. And all at once I experienced a mindless terror beyond all understanding.

'God is merciful, Horace - when He feels like it. God is endlessly cruel - when He feels like it. God creates; God destroys. God loves and protects; God hates and torments. Everything that *is*, good and bad, comes from God, and everything that has been, and ever will be, *is* God. Everything is His deserv*ed* plaything; His whim - His…toy.'

The Bishop pronounced the word *toy* in a curious, lingering, almost playful way.

'You are quite correct, Horace. God is an horrific, jealous, sadistic, merciless, entirely capricious being. And demons *are* everywhere,' he repeated. 'And they take many forms. And there are many ranks, from the highest to the lowest. And at the summit, Lord over all Creation, the highest ranked and greatest demon of them all, is God Himself, the Archdemon of archdemons, who for His own amusement manipulated the human spirit of an unremarkable working man, and called him Jesus, and convinced him that he was His son - the Son of God! And made of him a pathetic, gullible patsy. And put all manner of false ideas in his head, and false words in his mouth, and filled his mind with delusions, and sickly platitudes of love and mercy and forgiveness. And laughed at his meaningless death upon the cross, and at the gorgeous fiction of his resurrection.'

And at this the Bishop put back his head and laughed like a beast tormented by the moon.

I may have been screaming, and the next moment in blind panic I was clawing at the doorknob, willing the door to open. Then I ran, sweating and stumbling, from the Bishop's Palace and its grounds. I found blood pouring from my fingertips. I ran until I arrived in the village, practically delirious, where everyone I encountered stopped and stared at this raving madman. A bus was about to leave from the market square. I jumped aboard and it pulled away. I left everything behind.

This was three days ago. A lifetime. I don't know if anywhere is safe now. All my instincts tell me probably not. I will be pursued and silenced, because now I know the truth. And the truth beyond the truth is that there is no escape, either in this life or the next.

Booking in Advance

I look in the mirror and I think, that's not me. Whoever or whatever that is looking back at me, it's not me. That is nobody I know. In fact it's nobody and nothing, full stop. It's true I sometimes think I vaguely recognize whatever it is that somewhat balefully regards me from the mirror. But in any case that poor emaciated thing has nothing whatsoever to do with me. It's presumably some kind of malevolent spectre or wraith that appears from time to time. But, I repeat, it has nothing to do with me, with who I am (or was).

I decided to try to escape this apparition. So I booked a train, to Woking of all places. It was the most anonymous destination I could come up with off the top of my head. To get to the station, three miles from where I live, I caught a bus. After paying the fare I climbed the stairs to the top deck, stopping to hold on a couple of times as the bus jolted. Then made my way down the aisle.

Normally on damp and humid mornings such as this all the windows upstairs are steamed up, due to none of the small upper windows being open. So all my fellow passengers are customarily sitting there like crash test dummies, staring at their phones, breathing in each other's exhaled breath, having apparently learnt nothing from COVID about disease transmission and the need for ventilation in enclosed spaces, preferring instead to lay themselves open to any virus or bacterial infection doing the rounds, even as they stare blankly at TikTok or puzzle games or banal texts from some new 'friend' they met but barely recall from the night before.

All of this is by the way, except to illustrate how different things were on this particular morning. For a start all the windows that could be opened were open. But more significantly nobody was looking at their phone, which was an all-time first in my experience. I was met by a palpable wave of hostility - not directed at me specifically, it was just in the air, everywhere. Everyone was staring at somebody else with undisguised malice, sometimes directly back at the person staring at them, so there'd be a staring contest of maybe ten to fifteen seconds, or else staring at someone whose rancorous gaze was boring into a third party's unsuspecting head.

Then, in the case of a direct confrontation, and without any visible concession from either side, the focus of spite and antagonism from each would switch to a different target. And so it went on for the entire length of the fifteen minute journey. It was all quite inexplicable, and frankly I was glad to get off at the station and see the bus set off again and trundle up the road with its cargo of bile and bitterness.

I found the platform and showed my prebooked ticket on my phone to the ticket inspector (or whatever it is they're called nowadays). It was then I got a nasty surprise.

'I'm sorry, sir, I'm afraid that due to recent changes in the operating conditions of the service provider for this journey, any prebooked tickets now expire before the due travel date.'

'What?'

'Your ticket is no longer valid for this service.'

'But...but look, here's the ticket on my phone - you can see clearly that it's the correct ticket for this journey. And there's my train, just over there, if you'd just let me get on it.'

'I'm sorry, sir, I can't do that. The train is full.'

'This literally makes no sense whatsoever,' my voice rising in anguish and anger. 'Why can't I just get on and take my seat - the seat I've paid for? Look, look - here's the seat number on my ticket, reserved specifically for me. That's the whole point of prebooking.'

'I understand that, sir, but this is a new policy designed to eliminate overcrowding. If you'd booked the same day, preferably just before the start of the journey, there'd have been no problem. If seats were still available at that point, the system would have allocated one of those seats to you.'

'But I have been allocated a seat, as I've just proved to you. That's the whole point of booking in advance.'

'Unfortunately that's not how it works, according to the revised terms and conditions of the service provider. I'm sorry, sir, I regret I cannot allow you on the train.'

'They're hardly a service provider if they fail to provide the basic service of reserving and holding seats for people who prebook,' was my ineffectual parting shot.

I thought of adding a few more unsolicited observations on the drawbacks to this new system, but by this time I'd run out of energy and will to argue my case any further, especially as by now we were surrounded by a crowd of interested onlookers enjoying the scene.

So I went back home, without further incident, to face once more whatever it was looking back at me from the mirror.

Difficulty in Crossing a Road

I have tried and failed a dozen times or more. Approached, retreated, approached, retreated once more, hesitated, waited, shuffled my feet, wiped my nose, dried my glasses, looked up and down the street, taken in the church spires and the top of the shopping centre in the distance and the tall tenements either side of the road curving in stately grandeur before straightening and falling away like a series of descending cadences, begun to approach, retreated once again, meditated on the streetlamps and lights coming on in flats above and shops below and all the people within at varying stages of their miserable lives, made up my mind that at last it was time to approach. But yet again ended up retreating to my default position.

Chief among the combination of factors ranged against me is the rain, light a few minutes ago but become increasingly heavy, which in itself and especially its effect on my glasses obscures my vision sufficiently that judgment of opportunity to even begin to successfully approach and cross the road becomes near impossible. Then there is the question of the volume of traffic on the pavement at this ravening hour of early evening. People walking, noisily, silently, stealthily, openly, singly, in pairs, in groups, men, women and everything in between, children, dogs, babies, prams, pushchairs, wheelchairs, bicycles, electric scooters, drunks, druggies, the indeterminate belligerents (common enough on a Saturday night), the bearded, the beardless, the thoughtful, the thoughtless, the profligate, the careful, the generous, the miserly, the psychotic, the sympathetic, the symbiotic, the single-minded, all swell and swirl like flotsam on the surface of a brackish river. And all impede and obstruct my increasingly desperate attempts to find an opening.

Then there's the cycle lane - an additional extreme hazard - whose denizens tear along as if on a mission from God, heads down, glaring intently, furiously driven, pinging wildly, intolerant, entitled, swaying, swerving theatrically, a world unto itself, morally unimpeachable, irreproachable, hands washed clean of all culpability, beyond rebuke, a movable feast, a moving altar, a plea and prayer to a sustainable future. But still, withal, presenting a significant danger to life and limb, requiring a lengthy pause, checking and rechecking in the failing light, with the lights of the crossing beckoning, heralding the road just beyond.

But having by some miracle got this far, the lights at this very moment turn against me, and once again the way is barred. A three-way junction, a system of Machiavellian complexity involving cars, vans, trucks, buses, cycles, trams, pedestrians, dogs etc. etc. in various labyrinthine orders of precedence. I press the button out of mere habit. But, cold, soaked and defeated, to escape the blinding rain and against the ever-present hazards of wheel and foot, I retreat once more to my sheltering spot in the trash-filled, graffiti-encrusted doorway. And so the process begins anew, and still the gloomy partially-lit tenements continue to cascade down the broad, rain-lashed road as if carried helplessly by the force of a superior will.

The Fly

I'd decided to seek the peace and calm of the park, an oasis of shady paths through manicured lawns and mature trees in full leaf. At least partly as a restorative following a frustrating, wasted hour after breakfast, during which I'd been prey to a feeling of unspecified foreboding.

I began to make my way around a group of clustered prams and pushchairs, smiling pleasantly to each nanny in turn as I passed. Glancing for no particular reason to my left I caught sight of a nanny who I happened to know slightly through a business connection with the father of the child in her charge. A pleasing, softly-spoken young woman. We chatted for a few minutes.

Then for some reason my attention was drawn to the child in the pram. A pretty child, just a year old, with a round angelic face, wispy white-blonde hair and startling blue eyes. Eyes that were now fixed on mine with what seemed for all the world like an accusing glare. Abruptly and without warning her head grew to seven or eight times its normal size to become the head of a gigantic fly. Its eyes, in proportion with the head, were enormous and terrifying, huge red near-hemispheres regarding me ominously. Stiff black bristles stood up in profusion around its head and body, and easily visible were the antennae and vibrissae.

Without warning a shower of sticky saliva drenched me, and before I knew it the fly had sucked up and consumed me as if I'd been a tiny speck of food. And at this point I cease to have any corporeal existence.

The Secret

At some point in the recent past I did something so terrible my mind rebels against memory. In fact I recall no details at all except that it was something unimaginably bad. I wake up screaming, drenched in sweat, hoping against hope that it didn't really happen. I jump up, staring about me wildly in the shock of half-remembrance, trying to grasp the exact nature of the thing I've done, or think I've done. But like a shadow withdrawing behind a pillar, the instant I turn to look, it's gone. Sometimes I think I can almost grasp the nature of what was clearly a grossly inhuman act, while simultaneously averting my gaze in horror and panicked denial. Is it really possible that I actually - let's state it baldly - that I took someone's life? Killed them, murdered them, beat them to death, knifed them, hit them in the head from behind with a heavy hammer in some remote corner of the dark unknown. Yet still, unbelievably, I remain free, my heinous crime apparently undetected. Denying the fact (if fact it be) as far as possible to my conscious mind, somehow maintaining to all outward appearances the quotidian forms and rituals of a normal, unremarkable life. Nevertheless fearing the dark hours of introspection and the stalking claims of evocation and the prospect of betrayal by my unconscious.

Yet nobody knows of this vile act but me - or so I assume. Nobody suspects I am anything other than what I appear to be. Having to bear this solitary burden, however, alone and unaided, is oppressive beyond words. While contending with and against the constant dread of revelation, there is a longing to share my shameful secret and so unburden myself. But is it even true, or simply some fantastical flight of paranoia casting false accusations, self-accusations? To know one way or the other would be something, a lessening of the burden. Or would it? To know for sure that in the depths of ebony night, the moon concealing behind a veil of dark cloud like layers of silk, I went out searching for prey like some animal predator stalking unseen through tall grasses. And then - and then the sudden lunge, and the committing of unspeakable brutality against innocent victim. Breaking through a wall of glass into a realm of sweating fear and festering guilt. But anyway, it may not have happened. It may not have happened.

The Hall

In those deceptively bright, naïve, sunlit days of the mid-1930s, when fascism was on the march all over Europe, a stoical cart driver made her way slowly on her delivery round, occasionally chiding the horse good-humouredly for lack of effort. Beyond the factories, begrimed bricks by the tens of thousands in repeating patterns, the familiar thudding and hammering and whirring and rattling from within. Beyond the ruined stone arches leading to the grove. Skies the texture and colour of a high wind, leaves like brittle fish occasionally pirouetting through the cool dead air, to land among others as if their landing place had been preordained.

A bell rang somewhere within the Hall, multi-gabled, with mullioned windows. Rumours of vampires and ghouls within the Hall, while unsubstantiated, remained rife. The cart driver waited at the lodge house, preferring to maintain a safe distance from the main house as long as possible. Debating within herself whether in fact to unload the goods there, no matter what instructions might be received.

A lock turned somewhere. Of course, goods delivered suggests corporeal beings - to me, at least. Flesh and blood. And the like. But what if through long and gloomy passageways, ill-lit antechambers, secret doors and hidden crypt buried deep underground elusive figures sometimes crept. It would be a surprise in such a building if some manifestation of the supernatural in some shadowy form or other did not lurk at certain times. The Hall itself, strangely, ominously, was without shadow in bright sunlight, at least according to some reports. Yet what use were goods delivered via cart and driver to non-corporeal beings? A distinct sinister presence within was often felt, once more according to rumour. Whether strictly human or otherwise remains unknown. Yet who or what inhabits the lodge house? Servant, acolyte, familiar? As storm clouds gather over Europe, still the cart remains, parked casually (as if there was nothing to fear) by the small stone lodge house.

Flamboyant Eternity

I'd thought it was meant to be teeming with rain that afternoon, the kind of rain that precludes vision further than, say, twenty or thirty yards ahead before encountering an impenetrable gloom. But I was clearly wrong, as it turned out to be one of those rare perfect days where, sitting in the back of the taxi as it wound steeply up towards my destination, the very air smelt more fresh and more perfumed, the sky more lyrical, and the brightly-coloured plants and bushes without name or form that practically threw themselves towards me in luxurious abandon were all more exquisitely imagined than anything I had ever experienced before.

At last I found myself standing at the foot of a flight of monumental stone steps that led up to the intricately wrought gates of my host's mansion, situated overlooking a lush landscape of startling beauty. I was feeling somewhat anxious, unsure of the reception awaiting me, but before I even had a chance to ring the bell the main door swung open, and there before me appeared this chunky Romeo, dripping with jewellery and evident goodwill, with a smile like the span of a bridge. It was so sincere it was almost slipping off his face. His warm and welcoming *Hellooo, darling*! was so damp with emotion it practically rattled the chandeliers. And what chandeliers!

They were everywhere, like wedding cakes of crystal suspended above our heads as we padded from room to ostentatious room, all crammed with priceless reproduction antiques, shimmering and sickly, each room a hall of mirrors, my host's face and smile reflecting from every polished surface of wood and marble, glass and gold, his smile smearing and scintillating in all directions in a riot of echo and emulation as he expounded on every detail in silken tones that left me with the feeling I'd just been force-fed an entire ten-course banquet.

It was altogether an otherworldly experience. And to think that all of this would endure (endure being the operative word) for the rest of Time - for all eternity - and the boundless shallows of his spirit in all its platitudinous sincerity would infuse my soul with such measureless devotion as to make us as one, forever and ever.

Harrogate 3440

The phone rang in the hall, a wonderfully mechanical yet musical sound from the old-fashioned black telephone, such as you never see or hear these days. Unusually, Rose was up, and she tottered slowly through from the living room to answer it.

'Harrogate 3440.' Her voice slow, deliberate, quavering.

'How are you, Rose?'

'Oh, it's You, God.'

'Are you keeping well? I expected Len to answer.'

'Are you really trying to tell me You don't know who's going to answer?'

'How is Len?'

'He's in bed. I've just brought him his dinner. A bowl of consommé and a few crackers and some cheese on a tray, if you must know. And keeping up the pretence that You are not omniscient and therefore know in advance everything I could possibly tell you is pointless - unless of course you're not, and *that* is the pretence.'

'How is Len?' He repeated.

'He's poorly, as well You know. He's got a chest infection. His breathing's laboured. It was attending that Armistice Day service in town a couple of weeks ago that did it. Two hours out in the freezing cold. I told him he was too old for all that sort of thing now and it would go to his chest, but he wouldn't listen, and he's not been well since.'

'He'll recover, this time, Rose. Don't worry yourself.'

'I will worry, if you don't mind. Anyhow, what do you want?'

'Neither of you are getting any younger, Rose. It's time to prepare for the inevitable. And I'm not talking about Len now.'

'What's that supposed to mean? Prepare for what?'

'Now, now, Rose, you know exactly what I mean. It's time you started to believe. It's the right thing to do.'

'I'll never believe.'

'You're very stubborn.'

'I'll never believe in You or Your supposed "good works". Not after what You did to me.'

'That was a medical emergency, Rose, and medical care back then wasn't what it is today.'

'Then what use are You? Tell me that. The poor little mite. That poor innocent little thing.' Becoming emotional, still, after all these years. 'What use are You, if you can't intervene for good when it really matters. Tell me that.'

'There wasn't a vaccine for diphtheria then. There was nothing anyone could have done. Not back then. And truth is you've made a good life, despite that, Rose. Len had a good career. You had more children.'

'She was my first, and You took her away, and it was a horrible death. I hate You. And I'll never believe.' Quietly sobbing now as she spoke. 'The little love. She'd just started to walk and explore things, and You let her be cut down.' Bitterness in her voice and through her sobbing, still, after all this time. 'Just go away. And don't ring this number again. I don't care what happens to me - I haven't cared this past fifty years. So save Your breath. Oh just get off the line. I'll never believe.'

And she rang off.

Creaking Jesus

It's always there. Just above me, creaking and cracking. Hobbling to and fro, to and fro. Busy with whatever revolting, meaningless activity it's currently perpetrating in its stinking lair. Creak, creak, creak, creak. Of course the paper-thin hardboard flooring is partly to blame. How on earth the builders of this place got away with that. Talk about pulling a fast one. Creak, creak. I call it Creaking Jesus, for no particular reason (apart from the creaking). One of the more repeatable soubriquets among a litany of things I call it. Creak, creak, crack, crack, creak, creak. Doesn't matter where I am, kitchen, bathroom, living room, lying in bed. Somehow it always manages to be directly above me creaking its way to well-deserved extinction.

I don't wish to appear unkind, but it can't come soon enough for me. Creak, creak, creak. You old fecker, stay in one place, for Christ's sake. You're not achieving anything, you're not going anywhere. You're just creaking to no purpose. Then, of course, inevitably, there's the TV. What violence I would love to commit against that TV. Or, especially, its owner. Both on a similar intellectual level. The TV maybe a little ahead. 6.50 AM it starts up, every goddam morning, Sundays included. The occasional relaxing lie-in? Forget it.

I keep my distance from these people, but sometimes interaction is unavoidable. I don't even know who most of them are. Is that him? That could be him. Could be any of them, to be honest. Never seen his face. That could be Creaking Jesus. Collapsed on a chair in the entrance lobby behind his walker, grotesque scrubby face behind thick glasses, bulging stomach mercifully shrouded by stained t-shirt. Says he's going to 'entertain' them in the lounge after they've all been fed and their stalls cleaned out. He's going to sing and play his guitar, currently balanced on his walker. Probably the same criminal who's 'on the decks' at the Xmas party.

On the decks! It's not the 1960s anymore, you creaking bastards. These godforsaken boomers, they think it's still 1967. Beads and beards, flower power, LSD, free love. Free love! You disgusting creaking decrepits, you thought you invented everything, including sex. You overprivileged overentitled boomers. Just be quiet, for God's sake. Just sit in a corner, don't say anything, and don't make any noise. You're here on sufferance, and don't forget it. You've had your go. And when, mercifully, your time is finally up, just leave quietly, and don't make a sound on your way out. Life, living is for the young.

On the decks. My God. But anyway that could be Creaking Jesus on the decks. In any case some dribbling, incontinent, stone-deaf wreck. Creak, creak. Take that, boomers. Everybody hates you. There'll be a national day of celebration when the last one is finally gone. Oh well (as they say), that's a snapshot of my life. An object lesson in endurance and futility. Existence really is a joke. It's a twelve-lane highway of banality. Creak, creak.

The Project

He was just an average, run-of-the-mill kind of guy. That's what his work colleagues thought when they thought of him at all, which was rarely. A little quiet, a little odd. Nothing more than that. Kind of anonymous. To his wife he was a kind, loving husband, patient, giving, the man of her dreams, even after twenty years of marriage. His son and daughter just thought of him as Dad, they didn't know any different. None of them, family or otherwise, had any idea how he felt inside.

What he felt. These days he felt nothing much unless it was quiet desperation. And boredom at his situation. There was not much in the way of solace anywhere or in anything. Unless maybe in hiking alone through the wilderness, escaping people, by and large. He'd often dreamed of an escape plan. An out. Something permanent, where he could disappear off-grid and out of sight, somewhere nobody could ever find him. If he could just think of one.

The desire to wipe everything away had been growing for years. Just to wipe the slate clean. Then he'd had the idea of a van. He'd watched a bunch of van life videos. That was an out.

So this is my first time doing this, filming myself...let me just...So there's not a lot left to do, it's pretty much done. I'll show you where I'm at and, pretty much give you a quick rundown on the whole project. I'll keep it short, probably no-one's going to want to hear me talkin, but it's not to post anyway...just for myself as a record.

So just to start at the start...I bought this van two years ago, just a regular knocked around Ford Econoline work van, still with all the signage on the body. All of which I've kept, as you can see. The firm went out of business, so that's all redundant. Only thing I've done is blank out the mobile number.

So the idea was for it to look like a regular work van no-one would look twice at...just checked the camera, just making sure the sound level was okay. Like I said, this is my first...hold on, let me just move a little over here where there's more light.

So yeah, the idea was for it to look like a regular everyday work van. A stealth van, undercover kind of thing. I wish now I'd kinda documented this whole thing, all the work on the van from the start. And also done all this in a lock-up somewhere instead of at home. That's an extra complication, now, too many people know about the van. I mean family, so yeah, that's a complication.

His childhood was a mess. Five siblings, he was the eldest. His father - he didn't remember much about him, and what he did wasn't pleasant - was gone by the time he was eight. Had wanted to make a man of him. 'Chucky boy, you gotta be able to take care of yourself, no-one else is gonna do it for you.' Well, he was right there. So he'd made Chuck (real name Charles Brown, known inevitably as Charlie Brown, which as an adult he regarded as a cruel imposition on a child) put on gloves and they'd spar in the backyard. If you could call it sparring, a brawny man delighting in beating the hell out of his son, cuts, broken lip, broken nose, bruising, blood, the works. Dazed and crying, while his dad, thoroughly enjoying himself, tells his son to quit being such a big sissy.

Didn't really miss him after his mother, tearful, told him his father was gone - no explanation - and now he, Charlie, was the man of the house. She really took to the drink after that. Chuck hated the way his mother would tearfully beg him to give her a cuddle on the sofa, hating the warmth of her body as she held him tight, the odor of sweat, her straggling hair in his face, the smell of alcohol on her breath, smoothing his hair, caressing his face. He took some consolation from taking his duties as 'man of the house' seriously, ordering his siblings around, three boys, two girls, handing out beatings if they didn't do his bidding, girls included, delighting in the yowling and screaming.

They moved as a family several times, each place worse than the last. Even at that age he dreamed of escaping, of moving west, to Wyoming or the Dakotas. Big, empty states. Free from people, for the most part. Just the sound of the wind and faraway horizons. A little wooden shack, smoke rising from the chimney. Stacked full of provisions. Everything he needed.

I've had a pretty shitty life, and pretty much always hated the way I look. So frickin ugly. Probably why I didn't film the conversion from the start, having to look at my own frickin ugly face. Double chin. Fat. Short. Bald. Christ. But I'm kind of getting used to seeing myself as other people see me. Guess you can get used to anything.

So let's take a look inside the van first, then I'll tell you about the safety improvements I've made. I guess first I should tell you about the van itself. It's a '97 Ford E-150 Econoline, a regular workhorse, and this has the 5.4L V8. I could have done with a bigger, more powerful engine, as I've put quite a bit more weight on the van as I'll show you later. But it's okay, and it was cheap, only a couple of thousand dollars. High mileage, but it works okay, and I can fix anything that needs doing. It's a little beaten up, you can see these scrape marks here, but that's fine, that's how I like it, looks like what it was used for most of its life, a truck used to being around construction sites. I've even put these lengths of industrial piping on top, which also hides the solar panels.

Okay, so inside, first I stripped everything out. Then insulated everywhere, every space I filled with insulation, the stuff made from recycled plastic bottles. Then over that sheets of sound deadening material. Then half inch plywood on the floor, back doors and ceiling, then cheap stretch carpet glued in place. Really insulates the van, doesn't look too pretty but stops any booming, really reduces noise. Installed all the electrical system myself, solar panels, everything. Built the bed myself, converts easy to a couch. Bought this memory foam mattress, so that goes on top of a plywood base. Kitchen sink with electric pump for the water, couple of six gallon jugs of fresh water. Works real nice. Work surfaces, made them all myself. Ceiling fan, recessed LED lights. Over-cab shelf for storage. Just got to finish off these storage cabinets, a little tidying up here and there, stock the van up with provisions, and it'll be pretty much done.

A stepfather arrived when Chuck was ten. His mother had had a few trial runs, but this one had stuck. Not that they'd married, stepfather was an honorary title. There were no beatings, only sly mockery, echoing the bullying at school on account of his looks. He'd just become aware he looked less than ideal, totally unattractive, misproportioned. Now it was all he could think of, draining any residual confidence. Shunning mirrors, hating his looks, himself, everything and everybody. His forehead was large and domed, so he wore his hair hanging down to mask it, his nose was long and thin, receding chin highlighting two protruding front teeth. In addition, his body was too long for his legs, so of course he was called Dwarfie. Or Peanut (on account of Charlie Brown). Or Stinkbomb. On top of everything his mother had never put hygiene, personal or otherwise, top of her list of priorities, so without being told to do so he rarely washed or showered. Dirty, unkempt, unattractive, he was generally shunned. 'Don't choose him, he stinks.'

Yeah, talkin of complications, that's the difficult part. Dealing with all that. I could have had this finished months ago, but my wife brings nothing into the house. Nothing stopping her working part-time, but according to her she has to be here when Mikey, who is fifteen, gets home. As if he needs or wants his mother hanging round him all the time. It's just a crazy situation. Total drain on me, my resources, everything. Wearing me down continually. But now, finally, there's an endpoint, and I've more or less accepted it, the need for it. It's been real difficult, but it's the only out that makes any sense. Like I say, I've pretty much accepted the need for it.

So…No-one understands the pressure I'm under, been under for years, the repetition, day after day, year after year, and for what, for nothing. Nobody understands the agony, it's a kind of torture, it's like a long scream into a vacuum, into total darkness, where nobody's listening, while I just go insane with boredom. Just freakin screaming inside of me with despair and boredom, and nobody's listening. Basically, what I'm going to do will stop the screaming, hopefully.

So….any doubts or anxieties about what I'm doing, or about to do, any anxieties I had…it's just a case of there's no rational alternative, it's all about putting a stop to the screaming in my head. Not just in my head. Everywhere.

Quite unexpectedly, in his twenties he'd met someone who fell in love with him and wanted to marry him. He went with the flow, accepted the momentum of events. But the very fact Marcie loved him, hateful and unlovable as he was in his own eyes, actually weighed against her. The very fact that she *still* apparently loves him, even now after twenty years of marriage, when he hates and despises himself, only increases the contempt he feels for her - for loving someone who is hateful - and only goes to prove she doesn't know a goddam thing. How can anyone say otherwise when she loves and values someone who is worthless? Makes no sense. The same internal argument applies to his children, with the added negative that they carry his genes. How can he feel anything for offspring who carry his DNA, and daily betray the fact in their looks? He can't so much as look at them without seeing himself and his glaring flaws. It's like being gratuitously confronted with his own defects.

An added factor, so far as his wife is concerned, is that she doesn't work, sees herself as a home-builder, whatever that's supposed to mean, bringing nothing in, draining his bank account, the money he makes working at the repair shop. Even now, when their youngest is fifteen, she has to be at home for when their almost adult children come home from school, giving them that sense of security so often absent in today's society of latch-key kids, according to her. As if she knows anything about it.

Now I think I'm maybe doing it all wrong. I mean the stealth approach. Okay fine if I was planning on hiding out in the city, but it's gonna stick out like a beacon if I head off into the wilds. Been better if the van had looked like all the other van lifers. And

I just watched a video where a guy's lived in a van for the past five years, parking in city streets, clearly a van life rig, and never had a problem. Key is to figure out where you're thinking of spending the night, then when you've chosen your spot, sleep - then go first thing in the morning. Don't start making breakfast, doing your washing, walking the dog, whatever, just go, and don't come back to the same place. Then nobody'll notice you or bother you. Live and learn. Maybe I'll paint over the signage. It's all a process. And then when I do what has to be done, and then set off, I guess I'll keep on learning as I go along.

He'd lost interest in sex some years ago, not just with his wife, but with anyone. In fact the very thought made him sick. But even before he felt that way he'd never tried to have an affair, just assuming he was too unattractive to interest anyone. He disliked the dependence on another person that a sexual relationship implied, especially someone he didn't love or respect. His fantasies were entirely asexual, revolving around the myth of the lone hero, the man who stands alone, complete in himself, depending on no-one. The hunter, the lone warrior, the solitary outdoorsman. And though he had sufficient self-knowledge to realise how far short he fell from this ideal, still he aspired to it.

His wife expressed no blame towards him for his withdrawal, only complete understanding, blaming herself and the fact that she'd suffered from depression for years, and that she'd allowed herself to become overweight, not to mention moving into middle age and the inevitable loss of looks. Of course all this had made her unattractive to him. She understood. He didn't care that she was fat. Or middle-aged. But her ignorance of his true motivation for sleeping in the spare bedroom only served to ramp up his contempt, coupled with increasing irritation at the drain on his resources, when all his energy and every last dime of his income should have been directed towards the project.

I'm such a frickin loser. I can't even get the frickin van right. Just tested the electrics and there's some problem with the solar power controller, it's somehow tripping the isolator and…anyway, I'll get it fixed. That's not why I wanted to do this video, but anyway I guess there's bound to be teething problems. What I didn't tell you earlier, before I put in all the sound deadening and fitted the insulation panels, I installed Kevlar ballistic panels. I don't know what's going to happen when I do what's gotta be done, but this stuff is bulletproof, so I'm gonna have some kind of protection, if and when everything kicks off.

Not only that, but I've fitted runflat tires. You can see they don't look too different, but say they've taken a few bullets and the tire's deflated, you can keep driving in safety for fifty or sixty miles. Way it works is when the tire itself has flattened due to deflation there's a roller or band within the tire so you're not running on the rim, as well as it keeps the tire on the rim. I haven't tested them, they're pretty expensive, but with the tire safely on the rim, the vehicle is supposed to have sufficient traction that you can drive away from danger and get to safety.

Last safety feature I fitted - all this stuff adds a load of weight, by the way, so like I said before I wish now I'd opted for a more powerful engine. Anyway, I've had the van fitted with bulletproof glass. It's top grade, protects against high velocity rifle fire. You can't really tell just by lookin at it. Something else I forgot to mention, I've put Kevlar panels in the engine bay around the engine, just to give the engine some protection, at least from the sides.

He was trapped in an uncomfortable, awkward, ugly, sweaty, stinking body which he hated. Escape was the only option. Escaping alone was the only way. He had to be free of encumbrances. Which meant his wife Marcie, and his daughter Loren and son Mikey. It was unfortunate, but what he had to do was necessary, just to be free, to shed the load, the crushing weight he'd been under for years.

Marcie, in her forties, still in love with the idea of being in love, and happy to adjust reality to fit with that notion. A somewhat foolish, frivolous woman who hadn't worked for years due to self-diagnosed depression. Chuck had financed her artistic ambitions, really just a hobby that ended up costing money rather than making any. She called herself an artist, and had a 'studio' where she'd paint anodyne, amateurish water colors of subjects such as puppies and kittens gamboling amid brightly colored flowers, sentimental cottages, butterflies, lurid sunsets. She'd sell originals, numbered prints (framed) and cards in an online shop, though the cost of materials far outweighed the tiny number sold. She'd post images of her creations on Facebook, and family and friends would dutifully enthuse over them. And she'd tell people about her wonderful husband who was always buying her materials and brushes and frames and books about paintings and artists. He was just the best husband. Such a kind, nice, sweet guy, gets a little moody sometimes, but never really blows up. She just waited for the bad moods to pass, then he was back to normal again. But he would always do anything for her, had always supported her through her depressions. He was just the best.

As for Loren and Mikey, they were really good kids, and she was really proud of them. Loren would be starting college soon, majoring in psychology, had a long-term boyfriend, just a clever, kind, sweet girl, she was so proud of her. Loren was outgoing, Mikey the opposite, very quiet, spent long periods in his room playing video games. Roleplay fantasy type stuff. Never any trouble, either of them. Just really good kids. And the nicest thing was, physically they always reminded her of Chuck. Something about the eyes, or the chin, or maybe the nose, just a general look about them which reminded her of her husband, and that was nice.

Okay, well I guess this is it. The van's finished, fueled up and fully provisioned. I don't mind the idea of being on the run, if that's what it comes to. Hiding out, maybe a shootout if I get trapped somewhere. I've got an assortment of weapons stashed in the van, and I know how to use them all, plenty of ammunition. The van's prepared, semi-armored, good to go. I've stockpiled it with provisions, simple stuff, cans, dried food, stuff that'll keep for months, gives me options to hide out in different places. If it's a chase, at least the van's armored, so I'll have a chance to get away, then hole out someplace. It's all a matter of chance. Hopefully I'll get a head start of at least a few days, maybe a week or two. Who knows.

If I can reach somewhere remote I can maybe just disappear, maybe switch vans at some point. Even change my identity, grow a beard or something, change my name. It's all moot at this point. First I gotta do what's got to be done. I'm not looking forward to it, but I'm pretty much reconciled to it now, it's really my only option. And once I hit the road and we're on the way, hopefully I'll start to feel a little better, bit by bit. Find some peace, solitude, get away from other people. Hopefully then the screaming inside my head will stop. At the moment it's difficult to imagine. When you're in the middle of something, kinda like being in prison and you've been there for years, it's difficult to think what it would be like outside.

And if it all goes wrong, and for whatever reason I'm, you know, surrounded or whatever, well I can just use one of my handguns and put a hole in my head. And I'm fine with that. I'd get peace that way just the same so it's pretty much the same difference.

Van lifer Charlie Brown dies after 50 mile police chase

Van lifer and suspected killer Charlie 'Chuck' Brown died yesterday surrounded by a SWAT team after a 50 mile chase.

Brown, 46, an auto technician from St Louis, Missouri, is the prime suspect in the brutal slayings of wife Marcie (44), daughter Loren (18) and son Mikey (15).

They were found dead two days ago in the family home in Breckenridge Hills. Each had died of a single gunshot wound to the back of the head.

'It appears all three were asleep in bed when they were killed,' said police spokesperson Sgt Christine Pierce.

Police believe that the cold-blooded gangland-style executions were committed with a silenced weapon to avoid waking each subsequent victim.

Brown's van was spotted at an RV park in Wessington Springs, South Dakota. It was easily identifiable due to the signage of a defunct business still on the van.

Officers found images of the vehicle on a flash drive inside the house where the murders took place. The flash drive also contained detailed plans, including a list of RV parks in South Dakota.

'Finding the flash drive was crucial,' said Sgt Pierce. 'It saved critical time in tracking down our suspect, and gave us a list of likely locations to search.'

According to police reports, the suspected killer must have been watching for the police. Seeing the SWAT team vehicles entering the RV park, Brown somehow managed to evade them, and a chase ensued.

Finally, just the other side of Big Bend Dam, the pursuing vehicles were able to force the heavily-armored Ford Econoline van to a halt. Seconds later several shots were heard. Brown's blood-splattered body was found in the van alongside a pistol.

Androphobia

Alice knew she was diminished, how diminished she'd become, even as she was clear that events had made her so, and that it was none of her doing.

She had only two clear memories of her father - a menacing, bearded figure - one of him and her in her bedroom, and one in a café somewhere involving an altercation with a stranger. Both had involved intimidation and violence.

He'd left for good before her fourth birthday, yet these recollections of a monster looming fully-formed out of her nightmares were so powerful, they were all she could recall from those earliest years.

As she entered her teens, these fleeting memories seemed if anything to grow in power, a trigger that left her sweating, nauseous and shaking in fear.

Eventually, in her early twenties, she'd manage to construct, through self-therapy and will-power, a mental defense mechanism that deflected and diffused the terror before it could take hold. It was a tactic that usually worked, and from that point of view her life improved, though the failure to address the root of the problem came at a cost.

After he was gone permanently, her mother, older sister and herself had become a self-protective unit, a triangle of power, admitting no-one into the inner sanctum of their mutual support system. Their mother never had any further partner or boyfriend, to her daughters' knowledge.

In the following years, up to the start of puberty, Alice managed to control her fear of the opposite sex. At primary school she contrived to ignore, completely shut out the rowdier elements, and even managed to have friendships with one or two boys her own age, gentle, softly-spoken souls she could treat as honorary girls.

Not that all girls were pleasant, of course, but even the most unfriendly or spiteful never filled her with that familiar breathless anxiety.

Things started to escalate when she moved up to high school, where the majority of teachers were men. Sitting at her desk waiting for the teacher to appear, sick with anxiety. Then when he walked in, dizziness, disorientation that rendered her mute, unable to think or concentrate on anything but her fear. And if he was bearded, the fear was almost overwhelming, leaving her unable so much as to look at his face, still less engage or respond to questions.

If she could just make it through to the break, that was often as much as she was able to endure. At the first opportunity she'd slip away from the school grounds as unobtrusively as possible and play truant for the rest of the day, walk into town, have dinner in a cafe or buy a sandwich and sit on a bench, then spend a couple of hours at the amusement arcade before making her way home. Or else she'd go home earlier, knowing her mother would be at work and her sister still at school.

Sometimes she couldn't wait for the break, abruptly bolting for the classroom door following a tension-wracked ten or fifteen minutes with all her focus directed on reaching it, as if she were trapped in a prison cell and the cell door had somehow been left unlocked and unguarded, and this was her only chance and only gateway to freedom. Building up her nerve to scrape back her chair, grab her bag and make a run for it, all in one swift movement while the teacher's back was turned.

Of course this was unsustainable. Alice's mother received several phone calls from the school informing her of her daughter's truancies. Each time she'd talked with Alice, and each time been told it was a one-off, she'd just had a difficult day, it wouldn't happen again, she was sorry, she hadn't meant to worry or upset her. And no, nothing was wrong.

Now she'd been told that Alice had walked out of school earlier that day, her current whereabouts unknown. She immediately left work and drove through the town on her way home, hoping to catch sight of her daughter.

She put the key in the lock, turned it, and quietly opened the door. Listening, gauging the atmosphere of the house. Meanwhile trying to contain her anxiety and fear, when dark thoughts had inevitably kept intruding on the drive back from work. She had to remain calm and focused, for Alice's sake, for as long as humanly possible.

The house was warm, though the heating appeared to be turned off, and she took the fact that it was warm as a good sign. The house felt alive, welcoming. She thought Alice must be in the house somewhere. It was just a feeling. Irrational, of course. It was a positive thought to hold onto until proved otherwise, and she couldn't look beyond that.

She called out several times with no reply, but realised Alice might be wearing headphones. Putting all her focus on the task at hand she checked the living room and dining room, then the kitchen. That left upstairs. Out of nowhere came a thought that left her near faint with terror. She didn't know afterwards how she'd made it up the stairs to confront the possibility of her worst nightmare.

Into Alice's bedroom. There was the wardrobe. The doors were closed. She somehow knew it contained the answer, one way or the other, and apart from a quick glance paid no attention to the rest of the room. Each step towards the wardrobe brought her closer to screaming point, to being physically sick. With a supreme effort of will she steeled herself, then pulled both doors open in a sudden movement.

Instead of the horrific vision she'd fully expected, she found her daughter curled up at the bottom of the wardrobe among shoes and clothes, looking up at her with wide, frightened eyes. She collapsed onto her knees, weeping and sobbing in her joy and relief. She wasn't religious, but she thanked God again and again.

Alice felt awful, though she was relieved that everything was out in the open at last, and she no longer had to hide her agony. She hadn't intended for this to happen, to inflict suffering on her mother, of all people, which was why she'd never said anything about the terrors that afflicted her. She'd just been trying to hide from them, and everything.

Her mother rose to her feet and helped Alice from the wardrobe. They fell into each other's arms, and clutched each other and wept.

'Why didn't you tell me you were feeling like this?'

'I didn't want to bother you.'

'Oh Alice.'

They were sitting together on the sofa. Alice's mother had made them both cocoa. Steam was rising slowly in plumes and whorls from each mug in a comforting and reassuring way.

'I don't want to go back.'

'To school?'

Alice nodded.

'Okay,' said her mother, after several long moments consideration.

Alice looked at her mother as though she'd just seen the promised land.

'You really mean I don't have to?'

'Yes, you don't have to. We'll work something out. You're sure you're not being bullied or anything?'

'No, I told you, it's nothing like that. It's like I said, I just can't bear to be around men, or older boys. It makes me feel sick and dizzy. I just have to get away.'

'So it makes you feel frightened, being with men or around men?'

'Yes.'

Alice's mother took a thoughtful sip of her drink.

'I wonder,' she began tentatively, 'if we should, you know, see if we can get some form of counselling, just to see if we can - '

'I don't want counselling.'

'It's not a stigma or a judgement on you, or anything like that. It would just be a helping hand. You can't spend the rest of your life avoiding men, not looking at them, not speaking to them.'

'Why not?'

'Alice.'

'I hate them. I don't want anything to do with them.'

'But not all men are alike. And anyway you can't spend you entire future existence in a bubble.'

'I can try.'

A long pause.

'I really thought we'd put the past behind us now.'

'I'm sorry.'

'No, darling,' hugging her daughter once more, holding her tightly. 'It's not you. You've both been wonderful. In fact we've all done our best. We've all done well. We've been a team. We just need to find the best way forward, and we will.'

A schedule of home schooling was duly arranged and agreed with the local authority. Alice's mother negotiated working from home as much as possible, while Alice's grandma was happy to cover any gaps.

Alice did well academically, achieving a number of A-levels. She continued her education with the Open University, taking a degree in English and History, followed by a masters in English Literature. Her ultimate ambition was to write fiction, though her mother silently wondered what Alice would find to write about, given the circumscribed nature of her existence, cut off as she was from much of the world.

Although her defence mechanism allowed her to be in the same room as men (if it was a large room), or in the same shop (if it was a supermarket), or pass by them in the street, she was still unable to interact in any other way, refusing absolutely to have a conversation with a man, or respond to a man if he spoke to her. If she encountered a male with a beard, she immediately looked away and began concentrating intently on one of various verbal rituals, repeating familiar forms of words, shielding her mind until the danger was passed. The modern trend for facial hair did her no favours in this respect.

And that was as much progress as she'd managed by her mid-twenties. She still lived with her mother, working at home as a freelance proof reader and editor, writing fiction in her spare time. She enjoyed her life, despite its limitations. And who knows what prospects and pleasures might await her in the future.

A Sunny Morning

'Many saints and citizens live in caves,' I said.
People turned around and stared at me as if I was mad.
'Many saints and citizens live in caves,' I repeated. Then repeated it again and again, many times.
It was a busy street. Many people were going to and fro, maybe to work, or to jobs, or home. I don't know.
I noticed the time on a big clock on a building.
'It's ten to two,' I said, as people stared as they passed by. 'It's ten to two, ten to two, ten to two, ten to two. It's ten to two, ten to two, ten to two, ten to two, ten to two,' as fast as I could. Then I said it slowly. 'It's ten to two.'
People kept staring as they passed by to work or to jobs or home.
I thought I'd say it fifty times, 'It's ten to two, ten to two, ten to two, ten to two,' but I lost count somewhere around thirty, I think.
'It's a sunny morning,' I called out to the people passing by. Because it was.
'It's sunny today. It's a sunny morning', I called out. The people passing by still stared at me for some reason. I don't know why. They're probably just people with a lot of curiosity. There's nothing wrong with that. There's nothing particularly wrong with people that are curious.
'It's sunny today. It's a sunny morning.'
People passing by stared at me for some reason.

Then I saw a pigeon. Two pigeons.

'Look, there's two pigeons,' I called out. 'No, there's three pigeons, there's four pigeons. Look, there's five pigeons.'

People passing by stared at me for some reason. They were just next to a statue. The pigeons, I mean. I sometimes think it would be good if statues came to life.

It was getting hot.

'It's sunny today,' I called out. 'It's a sunny morning. It's getting hot.'

People passing by turned and stared at me. I don't know why.

The Loneliness of Traffic Lights

A traffic light at night is the loneliest of beings. Staring solemnly and with sorrowful intensity down some deserted roadway. Guardian of remote junctions and suspended roadworks in the early hours. Red the sternest and coldest yet saddest, most profoundly hopeless of its eyes. Yet stoical. There's never defeat in its unrelenting gaze, but also of course no hope. The pathos of its existence is heartrending. Standing utterly alone, unregarded and unloved, yet continuing to persevere when perseverance is pointless. Finally through red and amber to green. Yet no cars are passing. None are visible, none are heard or even expected. Back through amber, once more to red, this unflagging servant to public safety. No-one thinks of their unutterable loneliness until they've heard the concerted shrieks of despair from locations all over the city in the dead of night, rising and ululating, before dying down once more in broken sobs.

Chemical Romance

'Bus conductors.'
 'Winding gear.'
 'That's another one.'
 'Valderma.'
 'That's another one.'
 'Fairy Household Soap.'
 'Beware the unseeded Swede.'
 'That's another one.'
 'Coal tar soap.'
 'When it *was* coal tar.'
 'That's another one.'
 'Bournvita.'
 'That's another one.'
 'Pears soap.'
 'When it *was* Pears soap.'
 'That's another one.'
 'Spangles.'
 'That's another one.'
 'Beware the unseeded Swede.'
'I ought to try that sometime, together with all the other things I don't intend to try.'
 'No thank you and a half.'
 'Leaded petrol.'
 'That's another one.'
 'Two channels on the TV.'

'That's another one.'
'Wimbledon.'
'Chris Evert.'
'Long hot summers.'
'Breathless heat.'
'Strawberries and cream.'
'Sun-scorched courts.'
'High-bouncing ball.'
'That's another one.'
'Beware the unseeded Swede.'
'Corona lemonade.'
'That's another one.'
'Trams up the high street.'
'Izal medicated toilet tissue.'
'Beware the unseeded Swede.'

Two's Company

And she walks so slowly. Whatever is happening in front of her she fails to react. Or if eventually she does, it is with preternatural slowness. I lean alternately from one side to the other looking for a way past. But the path is narrow, and no easy opportunity opens up. I try lagging behind a few yards, then gradually quicken my stride, closing quickly, hoping to use this closing speed to step out at the last moment and pass. But it's all for nothing, no viable opportunity presents itself. And so we go on, with such little steps and at such a leaden pace, and yet relentlessly, inexorably.

As the day draws on and shadows like spectres start to gather and reach out from the cover of darkness, still we trudge. And still occasionally I look, though with fading hope, for some opportunity to pass. But by early morning I've given up all hope of having the path to myself and getting a clear run, resigned to my fate, reluctantly stoical, glumly accepting the apparent inevitability of my situation.

Into the night and through the night, still we plod, slowly, so slowly. And still, through force of habit and with no intention now of even attempting a pass, I lean from side to side - not so much around the curves and corners of the path, but along the straight sections where especially in darkness there is nothing to do or see, and even this leaning from one side to the other achieves nothing.

And so morning follows night, and night follows day, and still we walk. I suddenly sense, rather than observe, her steps begin to falter. How long has passed since we began? It seems like something that occurred in prehistory, so far back in time its very origins are now obscure. Her weariness becomes yet more apparent, our rate of progress yet more funereal.

Until one day as dawn was breaking, and grey forms began to emerge incrementally from the impenetrable moonless night, I lifted my eyes from where they had drooped in mortal weariness in contemplation of a spot on the path immediately in front of me. And saw that she was no longer there.

I almost stopped dead in shock and disbelief. When had she left the path? And where? Had she at some point simply toppled noiselessly off the pathway and in the stupor of my fatigue I had failed to notice?

What was clear was that, whatever the circumstances of her disappearance, I had at long last an open road in front of me, with no obstruction or hindrance. The path was mine, with not a soul in sight. Yet now, after so long being accustomed to follow, I found that my ambition couldn't be rekindled. It's so much easier to follow than to lead. And in any case what if someone comes up behind *me*, with more potential for speed, and now *I* am the obstruction?

My desire had evaporated, but there was still the path. And although, as I say, I feared someone coming up behind me, any alternative was unthinkable. So still I continue to walk the path, through wind and rain, and snow and storm, in sunshine and deepest shadow. And so far there's been no pursuing footsteps. I'll cross that bridge when I come to it.

A Matter of Supreme Importance

I received a short, terse letter from my solicitor. I was taken aback by its peremptory tone, but more than that disturbed and not a little surprised by its content. A matter had arisen which was so far-reaching in its consequences as far as my personal and especially business affairs were concerned, that it was a matter of absolute urgency that I consulted with the solicitor as soon as possible. Any delay in conferring would have the gravest consequences. So I lost no time in placing a call to the offices of the solicitor. It's a large firm with many solicitors on its staff, and a bittersweet feeling in the main lobby, no doubt due to the many cases effectively won and lost within its walls, the many lives destroyed, resurrected, put on hold, the aura of suffering and terminal ennui that permeates the very fabric of the building.

The solicitors tend to work in relays due to the pressure of work. When one drops from exhaustion another, regardless that their area of speciality may not match the unfortunate casualty, must step into the breach and field the ball. If they didn't, the whole intricate and interlocking mechanism would come to a screeching halt, with much high volume high density clashing of tortured gearwheels forced one against another in ways clearly not anticipated in their design. The entire system would probably jam up abruptly amid clouds of noxious-smelling smoke and cries and screams of anguish and despair, not to mention derailed career ladders. So the need for flexibility and the ability to multitask is paramount. Downsides, of course, being that any given solicitor may not necessarily be able to bring to a case the degree of expertise gained by working exclusively in a specific area over years, if not decades. And also for clients it's not always possible to enjoy the continuity and close working relationship vital in building a strong case - or very often even locate a specific solicitor within the building.

So I put in a call to the solicitor whose name was on the letter, and with whom I have had previous dealings. After a period of aimless meanderings around the seemingly infinite recorded options, an operator eventually answered and asked my business.

'I'd like to speak to Ms X, if possible. It's a matter of some urgency.'

'I'm afraid Ms X is in conference at present. Can I ask the nature of your inquiry?'

'I'm responding to a letter I received from Ms X in which she intimated the urgency of the matter.'

'Just a moment, please.'

I waited, my heart thumping, beginning to sweat, tapping my fingers rapidly on the desk to relieve my anxiety.

(If you wish to get no response at all for the next five minutes, please press 6.)

'Hello.'

'Yes, hello. Ms X?'

'Sorry to keep you. No, I'm sorry, you seem to have come through to the wrong department.'

'I was just speaking - '

'This is the - '

'No, sorry, go on.'

'This is the conveyancing department.'

'Okay, but just a few min - '

'Do you know which - '

'Sorry, go on.'

' - department you are wanting to speak to?'

'I'm wanting to speak to Ms X. It's a matter - '

'I believe - '

'Go on.'

'I believe she's in conference at present. But if you could just hold the line for a few moments, I'll see if I can put you through to the appropriate department.'

'Okay, thank you. That would be - '

(Alternatively, if you wish to experience severe and prolonged mental torture, please press 7.)

'Hello?'

'Hello?'

'Personal injury department. How may I help you?'

At this point my will was broken. So instead, after a day of recovery sitting quietly at home doing nothing, I decided to call into the offices in person, without an appointment, and trust to luck and determination. After several fruitless visits, unable to locate the solicitor, or indeed her office, I finally caught sight of her sitting on the roof of the building with several colleagues, apparently eating lunch. I tried to catch her attention by shouting and whistling, but she remained oblivious, consuming dainty white sandwiches (probably cucumber) and sipping on a plastic cup filled with (probably) red wine. Until quite suddenly, presumably having finished her lunch, she outstretched her white blouse-covered arms, and with a little upward leap soared away across the street to a nearby church steeple, narrowly avoiding the ministrations of a large black cat with glowing green eyes that had leapt up at her, claws unsheathed, as she'd started to ascend. In fact an army of cats had recently discovered the roof picnickers, and begun to make their lives hell.

For a while it seemed coexistence might be possible, bar the occasional violent incident. But gradually the cats through sheer weight of numbers started to take over the roof, while solicitors in greater and greater numbers could be seen, blouses and shirts fluttering like brilliant-white kites in the firmament, circling the roof, looking for an opening or vacant spot to roost, before soaring over to some nearby building, only to look wistfully back at their old offices. The building itself rapidly became completely overrun by cats, who had taken to mounting guards on the roof, and was now entirely devoid of solicitors, lawyers, paralegals, even clerks.

The solicitors never returned to the building. They are sometimes spotted, singly and in groups, high in the sky like pure white pocket handkerchiefs, scintillating as they catch the sun, released from the constraints of gravity and routine. Occasionally remnant sheets of legal documents pirouette down to earth, to be unceremoniously trodden in the gutter.

I never heard any more about the matter raised in the letter, and my instinct told me that it had probably been of no importance all along.

The Interrogation

For some reason I'd put my jumper into a woman's bag before the flight home. I can't remember now my motivation for doing so. I assume it was done deliberately, but even that supposition is unsupported by either hard facts or clear memory. I believe I have a memory of my action - or to put it more accurately I have a video clip in my mind of this supposed event that I can play at will, and it has all the appearance of reality.

Even before take-off I'd reached up into the overhead lockers and covertly - with perhaps just one side glance that nobody except a trained observer of human behaviour, a licensed clinical psychologist perhaps, trained in body language, with all their attention focused upon me, could possibly have noticed - placed my jumper - a beautiful, lightweight garment, silvery blue in colour, of purest cashmere - into a woman's capacious bag that she had already placed in the locker. Fortunately there was still space for my jumper, which I quickly concealed underneath various items, books, diary, white cardigan, suncream. Nobody could have detected the jumper without delving deeply into the bag. I had to lean over the woman in question - a middle-aged, overweight yet highly respectable matron already engrossed in a word puzzle in some magazine, peering intently through her glasses, frowning, pen held close to her mouth, absorbed in her activity.

I had no immediate cause for alarm when we landed. Disembarkation proceeded smoothly enough until I reached passport control. Then two stern-faced officials stepped in and required me to accompany them. I protested that my passport was clearly in order, and that I had luggage to collect, but my remonstrations were roundly ignored. I was taken into a large open-plan office. At each table immigration officers sat or stood with uniformly accusing expressions directed at the fearful unfortunate standing before them. At two of the tables stood two completely naked men. Atop each table, ominously enough, were a pair of rubber gloves and a bottle of massage oil, the sight of which did nothing to reduce my already sky-high anxiety levels.

I was taken to a table at the far end of the room. I can't remember now the substance of the interrogation, only that from the first it was hushed to the point of inaudibility, soon to become absolute silence. For five full minutes the only interaction, if it could be called such, was the hard, accusing stare of my interrogators boring into me. Until at last, at the very peak of a crescendo of tension, this front of steely impregnability began by increments to collapse. Their faces started to crumble, to lose form and substance, as if melting through the action of uncontrolled forces of inner emotional turmoil.

In an outbreak of what can only be described as mass hysteria, throughout the room people began openly weeping and sobbing. Even the naked men appeared to be affected. One of them threw himself to the ground in an apparent paroxysm, and then began to wriggle, wormlike, towards the door, in what seemed to me a blatant attempt at escape amidst the abandoned wailing and gushing of tears, a stratagem which disappointed me in its cold, self-serving artifice.

At last one of the officials reached down to an open drawer and, still sobbing, took from it the jumper I had hidden. He held it out to me, saying only, in a trembling voice, 'Take it, then.' I took it, thankful to have the jumper back in my possession, and proceeded to walk calmly from the room, glad to leave behind the cacophony of shrieking and chorus of tears.

And so I went home, well satisfied with my first experience of travelling abroad.

Too Tough

He was too tough to shield his eyes from the sun. Too tough to take a sip of water when desperately thirsty. He was too tough to shut doors after himself. Too tough to look in both directions when crossing the road. Too tough to acknowledge defeat. Too tough to stop smoking. Too tough to pick up after his dog. Too tough to trim his hedges or paint his downpipes. Too tough to acknowledge the pain when he slipped on ice and broke his wrist. Too tough to go to the hospital and have it set. Too tough to go to his GP when he experienced symptoms of lung cancer. Too tough to acknowledge his mortality when he died.

A Complete Mystery

Share your theories in the comments down below, love to see where you land on this one, pareidolia, scary, mysterious videos, share your opinions, love to hear your comments on this one, bewildered and unnerved, restless spirits, love to hear your theories, share them in the comments section down below, trending on socials right now, more questions than answers, captivating alure of the unknown, that no-one can quite answer, shrouded in mystery, epicentre of strange occurrences, defying rational explanation, power of suggestion, caught on CCTV, paranormal activity, rich tapestry, captivating and intriguing, remains a complete mystery, shadow figures, a trick of the light, optical illusion, camera glitch, let me know where you sit on this one, sparsely populated bed, strange circumstances and coincidences, unease and apprehension, sceptical of the paranormal, eerie footage, decide for yourself, unwanted negativity, replicate the anomaly, massive compilation, a glitch in the matrix, something more sinister catches our attention, and so it rolls on, or trolls on.

Speaking of which, are the dead apparently just mindless trolls? Zombie freaks pushing chairs around, sliding cups across surfaces, making cutlery fly, banging doors etc. It's all just pointless trolling. If, that is, ghosts and poltergeists are the remnant spirits of deceased humans. Is this purgatory they're sharing with us? And what of child ghosts. Are they condemned forever to remain children? No growth, no development, no hope of maturity? Wandering around in banal isolation, lost and abandoned forever. What kind of a god would allow that? I think we both know the answer to that one. So I'll leave it up to you, the reader, to decide. Are they human spirits, or are they something else entirely. If human, are they souls in purgatory? Does such a thing exist, and this apparent confinement within specific physical locations where once they lived (that is when still actually alive) represent their designated place of expiation? Their only means of expressing their agony to endlessly repeat a litany of banging, knocking, transportation of objects, playing hide and seek, and the production of various random noises. To troll endlessly until eventually (no doubt grudgingly) given the green light to pass through the Pearly Gates. Or are the forces behind these strange and unsettling occurrences something else entirely - perhaps infestations of evil, agents of the devil, demons? Or other forms of non-human entities, alien even, or maybe manifestations from an alternate or parallel universe? Or are they merely products of hysteria and paranoia with a spot of telekinesis thrown in to add verisimilitude, hallucinations somehow transformed or transmuted into visible and audible phenomena capable of being captured on camera?

Unsettling conclusion either way. Love to hear your thoughts in the head-scratching ghost-cleansing material escaped gorilla take a look at the many different mysterious circumstances possibly paranormal with sinister intentions, judge for yourself, petrifying figure semi-transparent a mystery to all who see it. Let me know where you land on this one in the comments down below.

You Expect Me to be Warm in Manner

I received a letter from an acquaintance for whom I have done a considerable amount of work, unpaid, gratis, a purely friendly, generous outpouring of energy. The letter signed merely KH. So that is my reward. A cool, cursory, offhand signing off.

   I was moreover disturbed by the manner of the writing itself in the handwritten note. There was something in the actual production of the letters which was peculiarly offensive, almost threatening in places. A violent slant to certain letters, capitals often emphatic, belligerent, whilst in contrast here and there words trailed off in a disinterested, unintelligible scrawl, a clearly calculated insult. The lines of the letter themselves were not even, nor evenly spaced, nor even reasonably parallel to the top and bottom of the sheet of writing paper, another obvious and deliberate affront. The whole affair reeked of an almost theatrical malevolence.

   Of course I have been wracking my brains trying to discover or deduce the motivation for this gross departure from common decency. All I can think of is the Christmas card I sent, back in early December. A harmless annual ritual, you might well suppose, with no hidden pitfalls. And yet, thinking back, I do wonder if there was, quite unwittingly, something untoward in the way I wrote the note, or even sealed the envelope.

Or was the postage stamp affixed incorrectly - at an awkward angle, perhaps - I don't recall it being so, and yet - or even - worst case scenario - had it somehow detached itself from the envelope, so that the recipient ended up bearing the full cost of postage? In any reasonable person that would surely provoke only the slightest irritation - or even wry amusement, and not the unmistakeable expression of malignant anger I was shocked to receive. Or were the brief lines of my message within the card not sufficiently straight? The ink not of the correct, or at least acceptable, shade of blue? Was the production of the letters of the words not passably neat and clear? The lines of the message straight one with another, and also in relation to the card? The message itself in any way unfriendly or condescending? Even if so, it would have been wholly unintentional.

And what of the picture on the front of the card. I had thought it to be inoffensive - a traditional, festive Christmas scene - carol singers gathered on a snowy evening around an open cottage doorway where an elderly couple stand smiling, light streaming forth in welcoming fashion on the friendly, excited faces of the singers, a Christmas tree, lit and decorated, visible through the cottage window, and in the background a line of picturesque cottages leading up a quaint lane to a fine old stone church, with a robin on a holly bush in the foreground completing the composition.

What could have been more wholesome than that. Yet something clearly happened to elicit the letter I received. And if not in response to the Christmas card, then what?

I've barely been able to sleep these past few nights, agonising over the whole business, wondering if I had inadvertently committed some unforgiveable social misstep. And yet, truth be told, it is of a pattern. How many of my friendships, or even just close business dealings, have collapsed in the wake of some communication with threatening overtones in the very shape of its letters and layout of the sentences, a frigid, hostile subtext to any actual meaning of the words.

And then, in the midst of all this and on top of everything, you still expect me to be warm in manner, when everyone else is cold?

The Time Traveller

'I've discovered the secret of time travel.'
'Okay.'
'You don't believe me?'
'I didn't say that.'
'So what's the problem?'
'There is no problem.'
'Go on, then, disbelieve.'
'I didn't say I disbelieve.'
'So you believe.'
'I didn't say that either.'
'You have to either believe or disbelieve.'
'Do I?'
'Don't you?'
'No, I could reserve judgement.'
'Until when?'
'Until I get more information.'
'You need more information.'
'All you've done is make a bald statement, and then try to push me into a corner - or rather one of two corners labelled, respectively, I believe, and I disbelieve. Firstly, that's unfair and unscientific. Secondly, to "believe" anything I need data.'
'You need data.'
'I need data.'
'What if I gave you more than data.'

'What do you mean?'
'What if I gave you hard proof.'
'That'd be nice.'
'I'm serious.'
'So you're going to demonstrate time travel to me.'
'More than demonstrate. If you're willing to come with me, I'll take you on the ride of your life.'
'You mean - '
'Yes, I mean I will transport you through time and space, to a specific time and place in what we erroneously refer to as the past.'
'So existence really is all a continuum.'
'That's right.'
'And you have single-handedly discovered the means of traversing this continuum and popping back to any specific point along it that you choose, with, I take it, complete accuracy and reliability?'
'Not back, but along.'
'Okay, along.'
'But otherwise, yes, that also is correct.'
'So, theoretically, we could go not back but along, and witness the birth of rock'n'roll at Sun studios in 1954. Or watch Don Bradman make a century at Lords. Or go not back but along to 1847 and ask Emily *Brontë* how her novel's coming along. Or go not back but along to - '
'Yes, we could do all of those things. But we're not going to. At least not this trip.'
'What a shame.'
'Instead we're going to go not back but along to 1967, and the workshop of an eminent though somewhat

elderly engineer who at that moment in time was or rather is developing a V8 engine for use in a sports touring car.'

'Why?'

'All will become clear in time. Meanwhile all you have to do is step into this cabinet.'

'This? It looks rather like a phone box.'

'They all say that.'

'Who?'

'Never mind. Now just step in.'

'I'd rather you stepped in first.'

'No, it wouldn't work that way.'

'Why not?'

'It just wouldn't.'

'Why?'

'I wouldn't be able to reach the controls.'

'What, you mean all these knobs and levers?'

'Don't touch those!'

'Why not?'

'Just get in.'

'Nothing will happen if I do, will it?'

'No, of course not. So just get in.'

'I'm not sure about this.'

'Nothing will happen, I assure you, until I touch the controls.'

'You're sure.'

'Quite sure.'

'You promise?'

'Yes, I promise.'

'Alright...I'm really not sure about this.'

'Just get in.'

'Oh alright…okay I'm in. What now?'

'Now I'm just going to shut the door quickly and turn this master switch.'

'Wait! I - '

My So-called Life

If I told you what my life was like you wouldn't believe it. Or maybe you would. I don't really care one way or the other. Anyway, odds are it'll end eventually. Hopefully soon. And thank Holy Matrimony for that. And please God let there be no afterlife. Let it end there where it ends. No comebacks, no encores. That being the very last thing I need or desire. Are you listening, God? Listen to me when I'm talking to you. What I'm asking is a perfectly reasonable, polite request, or series of connected requests - that you do not in fact exist, that there is no afterlife, and that therefore my godforsaken life can truly end when it ends and I don't have to spend the rest of eternity wandering aimlessly through a shadowland of endless knocking, door banging, plate throwing, and general moronic trolling.

Lord, in your mercy, hear my prayer.

The Doll

I picked the child up from where she lay huddled on the floor, sad and neglected. Her face as I held her was tear-stained and miserable. I held her to me and softly whispered endearments and consolations to show her that she was loved.

Later, a woman, tall, assured, smiling, walked past us into a glass-fronted office. The child out of curiosity followed her, tentatively pushed the glass door partially open and peeped inside. I thought the woman would greet her kindly and say a few friendly words. Instead of which there came a strange keening sound from the office, and the child quickly turned and ran back to me in shock and distress.

Angry and perturbed at this state of affairs, I strode to the office and pushed the door open with the intention of giving the woman a piece of my mind for needlessly upsetting a small and vulnerable child. Inside the office, instead of the desk I had expected to see with the woman sitting smugly behind it, was a large bed which almost filled the room. The bed was white, with white sheets and covers in some disarray, and drawers underneath for storage. There was no sign of the woman, yet the unpleasant keening noise continued.

I assumed that she must be hiding somewhere within the bed, either under the covers or possibly, somehow, in the drawers beneath, while continuing to make that disturbing noise in apparent mockery of a child's innocent curiosity. Then I noticed a doll lying on its back on the bed and realised with a jolt that this was where the keening was coming from.

As I looked at it, without warning the doll leapt to a new position on the headboard, from where it looked directly at me with its large piercing blue eyes. I ran from the office in terror, screaming.

The Little Fleckers

Mike and I were in the kitchen cooking up a storm for supper. We'd been tasked with keeping an eye on a couple of experimental robots, courtesy of the R&D department of our employer Robodevelopments Inc.

In our own eyes, and I know I speak for Mike here, we're just a couple of rough and ready cowpokes ready to turn our hands to any job the suits assign us to. So we didn't know anything about these new machines, hadn't been told anything much, except it was our job to babysit these two little fleckers (with contrived politeness we'd quickly named them Flecker 1 and Flecker 2) for a week or so.

'Just see what happens. See how you get on with them, and report back.'

'What's likely to happen?' said Mike suspiciously.

'Nothing bad,' smiled Dr Natalie Smith (a smile which never quite managed to reach her eyes), the lead engineer in charge of the project. She regarded us impassively and with about as much emotional engagement as if *we* were the robots - I'm not sure she made much of a distinction. 'Just relax and enjoy it. Pretend you've got a couple of buddies to hang out with for the week.'

'Sure, we'll have a real bull session, then play some cards, get some beers in, order some pizza!'

The distinct green eyes glinted, and the taut features kept in tension by hair pulled back and secured tightly at the back of her head seemed to tighten a notch or two further.

'When I said relax, I didn't mean don't take it seriously. These robots are a brand-new design, a giant leap forward from anything that's been seen before. Not in looks - they don't look remotely human, and that was never the point - but in terms of understanding and functionality, and the capacity and desire to learn. And we want to see how they perform in an everyday setting, interacting with ordinary people of average intelligence. Which is where you two come in.'

'Hey,' said Mike, 'I might be dumb, but that sounded quite a bit like an insult.'

'No,' said Natalie, 'I was giving you the benefit of the doubt.'

'Oh,' said Mike, grinning, 'well I guess that's okay then.'

'Think you can handle the assignment?'

'You mean do we think we can go a whole week without goofing up?'

Her mouth tightened this time, creating an ensemble with her hair and the rest of her face.

'I'm sure everything'll be just fine, doctor,' I said.

'Okay, good. Just don't...well, just don't...'

'In other words, don't fleck up,' said Mike, somehow this time managing to keep a straight face.

'What?'

'I meant to say, don't worry, boss, we won't let you down.'

She sighed, and thought, not for the first time, that it was only the human element that prevented society from moving on to a higher and better plane of existence - but this being a well-worn and utopian line of thought, she studiously repressed it.

We'd been allocated a detached house rented for the purpose in a typical suburban neighbourhood. There were three bedrooms on the first floor, one each for Mike and I, and one for the fleckers. The first night we'd roared with laughter at the comical sight of the robots laboriously climbing the stairs, line astern, having been informed by Mike that it was their bedtime. The second night we laughed less, and by the fourth night the very sight of the things filled us with disgust.

So after telling them (at an earlier and earlier time each evening), Time y'all went to bed now, go on, vamoose, git, we shut the living room door after them, shook our heads at each other out of combined relief and a shared abhorrence of our mechanical companions, then listened despite ourselves to the machines click and clack and tap up the stairs, across the landing and into their bedroom. Where the tap dancing continued for at least half an hour most nights before they finally quit.

'What in the hell are those things doing up there?'

I poured us a whiskey each with a hand which, though visually it didn't appear to be, I could swear was trembling - I guess it was just in my head. Then glared around wildly at nothing until the whiskey hit, at which point I seemed to calm down just a little bit. Just the noise of the things was literally driving me nuts.

'You'd think they'd just switch themselves off and sit in a corner on those godforsaken legs till morning. But oh no, they're dancing, or exercising or God knows what they're doing up there. What *are* they doing?'

'Beats me,' said Mike. 'Maybe we should go and take a peek. After all we're supposed to be observing and monitoring so we can report back.'

'Tomorrow. We'll do it tomorrow. I can't face seeing those goddam things again now we've finally gotten rid of them for the night.'

Of course the big problem was that we weren't aware of the little fleckers true capabilities until it was too late, and then some resentment towards Dr Smith set in at leaving us completely in the dark. As we found out later, these units were not just powered by sealed-for-life mini atomic reactors with huge energy reserves and a potential far beyond everyday requirements, but more than that they had a completely new type of synthetic brain developed by Dr Smith and her team with a near infinite capacity to learn, absorb information, develop and progress. The only thing they couldn't do was speak, which I guess was a deliberate choice on the part of Dr Smith.

So onto the fifth evening of the babysitting job, with the tension continuing to mount.

'Which one's that, Sherm?' said Mike, viewing the robots with a distaste now amounting to something approaching hatred. 'I can never tell the little fleckers apart.'

'Flecker 1. You can tell 'cos it's got this small section of black wiring the other one hasn't - just here. That's the only difference so far as I can see.'

As Natalie had said, they were not in any sense humanoid robots. More something like a spider crab - all legs, and then some. The shiny silver dome in the middle of their mainly black bodies contained the new wonder-brain which was at the heart of their supposedly huge latent capabilities.

So anyway like I said we were in the kitchen, cooking up a pair of fat, juicy steaks, and we had the fleckers for company. The room was pretty smoky with the frying but, beers in hand, neither of us minded much, and cared even less whether it might bother the fleckers, who though they couldn't speak, appeared to understand what was being said - at least, they gave the appearance of listening attentively at all times, and were capable of carrying out orders and instructions when given.

They were horrible things to look at and have around, their legs always making that distinctive ticking, clicking, tapping sound as they moved about. And I was getting increasingly nervous and irritated about being watched. It's an uncomfortable feeling knowing that a pair of eyes (or in the fleckers case multiple eyes) are following your every movement every second of the day. When I say multiple, these robots had six or seven eyes attached in various places on the top of their bodies. Eyes everywhere, just like a goddam spider, looking every which way. And when I say eyes, in fact they were more like the scope on a rifle, short, narrow tubes with a lens at one end, and fully articulated so they could swivel up and down and around a full 360 degrees.

Say you're standing there minding your own business, or trying to relax, or talking or whatever, at least one of these 'eyes' is continuously trained on you, even while the others might be swivelling here, there and everywhere, taking in whatever's happening, or if nothing's happening then God knows what they're looking at. I was continually wondering, what are these things even thinking about while they click and tap and clack, and swivel their goddam eyes in every direction at once. What in God's name are they even thinking about?

'I don't know if I can take much more of this.'

My voice came out as an anguished croak - maybe partly due to the smoke, though I'd just opened a window and it was clearing somewhat.

Mike paused in the process of forking the steaks onto our plates, to be followed by a pile of mashed sweet potato and a heap of coleslaw, to give me a questioning glance. My mouth would have been watering if it wasn't for Flecker 2 staring directly up at me with one of its tubular eyes.

'Why, what's up?' He continued to load our plates, pulling another couple of beers from the refrigerator.

'*That* goddam thing! It never takes its eyes off of me. Five goddam days, and it's never once taken its eyes off me. I tell you I just can't take being watched anymore. I'd like to tear its fricking - '

'C'mon, take it easy. Let's eat. We've only got two more days to put up with the little fleckers. Two days. File our report, then ten days' vacation. Two days, it'll go by just like - '

I was about to sit down, but as Mike broke off I followed the direction of his disbelieving stare. Even as he'd been talking, Flecker 1 had clicked, tapped and rattled over to the stove, opened the oven door and turned the oven on, presumably with a view to doing a little early evening baking.

'What in God's name is that godforsaken thing doing?' I almost screamed. My nerves were shot at this point.

'That's it,' shouted Mike. 'Leave that stove alone and get the hell on up to bed, the pair of you. Now, you hear me!'

They heard him, that much was clear. Ten, eleven, twelve eyes courtesy of both fleckers combined swiveled round and regarded Mike unflinchingly. But unlike previous occasions the robots failed this time to respond to a clear instruction. After a few moments Flecker 1 turned the majority of its eyes back to the stove, pulled a baking tray from the oven and put it up on a surface. Meanwhile Flecker 2 had clicked and clacked over to its companion and was standing beside it as if to give moral support, eyeballing us as it did so.

'Oh-ho,' said Mike, nodding and smiling a savagely ironic half-smile as he strode over towards the robots, 'it's like that, is it? Well, now, isn't that interesting.'

Bending over, bringing his head closer to them, he began to speak softly, just as if he was talking to recalcitrant children, and with just sufficient quiet menace in his voice to compel obedience - in the case of children. The robots, however, were a different proposition, apparently immune to Mike's intimidatory or persuasive power, and continued to ignore his now repeated instruction that whatever the hell's gotten into them, they better quit this nonsense immediately and get the hell on up to their bedroom.

After it became clear that, for whatever reason, they were set on defying our authority, Mike wandered back over to the table, still with our untouched plates on it and the sweet potato still steaming, and our eyes met in mutual tense anticipation of something about to give.

'Looks like we got a mutiny on our hands.'

'What are we going to do?'

Mike glanced over at the fleckers, a determined hostility in his eyes.

'D'you think we could lift them between us?'

'I don't know. I guess they're designed to be as light as possible. Maybe. What have you got in mind?'

'Lift or drag them upstairs one at a time and chuck them into their room. Maybe they'll stay there if we can manage to get them in there.'

'It's worth a shot, just to get those fricking things out of here.'

So first we picked up the cookery enthusiast, who offered no resistance, and discovered that it was much lighter than anticipated. Between us we could easily lift it, grabbing onto a couple of legs each, carrying it quickly up the stairs and depositing it with a satisfying thump onto the bedroom floor, shutting the door behind us. Then repeated the operation with Flecker 2.

Our supper finished, and feeling a little uneasy at hearing nothing from upstairs - no dancing, no calisthenics - we went up to check on our mechanical pals. And found the door locked. I rattled the handle and banged loudly. Not a peep from inside. I looked round at Mike and made the obvious remark.
　'They've locked us out.'
　'Well, we're just gonna have to break the door open, I guess. We can't leave them shut up in there doing God knows what.'
We began taking it in turns kicking the door in an attempt to smash the lock, or the door itself, but before we were able to break through and without warning something threw us back about ten or fifteen feet down the hallway. We lay sprawling, stunned, for however long, a good few seconds I guess. Then slowly got to our feet, rubbing our bruised limbs, gradually getting our breath back.
　'What in the name of Jesus Moses was that?'
　'Nuclear blast.'
　'What?'
　'A nuclear blast. It felt like a nuclear blast.'
　'When have you ever been in a nuclear blast?'
　'Okay, on a small scale.'
　'You wouldn't even be here if you had.'

'We gotta lure them out.'

'You okay, Mike? You seem a bit…'

'I'm good.'

We decided to have another go at the door. This time we got to within six feet of it, when we walked slam-bang into some kind of invisible barrier. At least, I did - I was just ahead of Mike, and received a hefty blow to my nose and forehead to go with the washing machine cycle we'd just been through.

'Ow! That fricking well hurt!' Rubbing my forehead, feeling an instant dull headache coming on. Concussion, prob'ly. 'What the hell is going on? What happened?'

'They've put up a forcefield. Don't ask me how, but those little schleppers have put up a forcefield. God, have we underestimated them.'

Shaking his head in disbelief.

'Great. Just great. So now what?'

A long silence.

'We need to lure them out somehow.'

'How?'

'Beats me.'

I walked forwards in the direction of the door, arm outstretched - only to discover the forcefield was no longer operating.

'Mike, it's down.'

Mike tested it for himself, and so we found ourselves standing right by the door again.

'What if it's them trying to lure *us* in,' I said, quietly as I could so the fleckers wouldn't overhear, 'and then they zap us again? What if they were going easy last time? We don't really know what these things are capable of.'

'A hell of a lot more than we were told by Nat.'

'Yeah, I'm gonna have something to say to her next time I see her.'

'Hey, I got an idea. What if we put something at the top of the stairs - a rolling pin, say - so when one of them tries to come downstairs it slips on the pin, falls downstairs and smashes itself to bits, hopefully.'

'What do you think this is, a two-reel comedy?'

'Sounds about right, way things are going,' muttered Mike. 'But seriously, Sherm - '

'No!'

'Look, the eyes those things have, in the position they're in, I'm not sure they can see immediately in front of them. Isn't it at least worth a try?'

'No, it isn't. The chances of an obvious set-up like that working are a million to one against. We're faced with something far more intelligent than at least one of us.'

'Hey.'

'I didn't say which one.'

'Say, what if they escape out the window?'

'Yeah? How are they going to climb down to the ground?'

'We don't know what they can do. Look, all I know is this is all-out war now. It's them or us. And I'm not taking any chances. If they got out the window they could take us by surprise coming in from the outside.'

'Okay, just to satisfy you, let's check outside and see if they're up to anything. Then at least we've got a better idea of what we're faced with.'

We checked outside, looking up at the fleckers window. The light was on, but otherwise there was no sign of activity. Back in the living room Mike went straight over to the wooden gun cabinet nestling in a corner.

'We need these,' he said. 'We need some firepower of our own against those mechanical nutjobs.'

'What good's a rifle against something capable of putting up a forcefield?'

'Maybe they can't keep up the forcefield for more than a minute or two at a time. They have to have some limitations. If we're armed and ready when they come out that room - and they gotta come out sometime - then maybe we can get the jump on 'em.'

'So what are we going to do - break into the cabinet?'

'Yep. That's just what we're gonna do.'

It took a while, but eventually we did manage to break in and grab a rifle each and some ammunition. We took up defensive positions - me at the head of the stairs, Mike just around a corner along the hallway. And then we waited.

And waited. Hours went by with neither sight nor sound. Then, at last, the click of a key being turned, the turning of the door knob, and the creak of the door slowly opening. The adrenaline was flowing, my heart thumping, Mike and I on high alert, primed and ready.

One of the fleckers tentatively tapped and clacked forwards just far enough that several of its legs were poking out into the hallway, and more importantly a number of its eyes were able to swivel around and scope out the situation. And then everything happened real fast. With a series of deafening bangs in the confined space Mike fired a number of shots in quick succession at the flecker. I saw at least a couple of its eyes shattered, bits flying up everywhere, before ducking down, fearing a ricochet off the metal body of the robot.

Then came shouting and the sound of multiple heavy footsteps from downstairs, and then the noise of boots clattering up the stairs as a Robodevelopments security detail of six men in grey uniforms, body armor, helmets and gas masks came charging up, with Dr Natalie Smith close behind. They quickly disarmed me and Mike as Dr Smith went over to the robot that been hit, reached down and deactivated it. The machine sagged down to the floor and remained there motionless.

Then she turned to us who, initially pinned down by members of the security detail, had been released on a word from Dr Smith. We stood together in the hallway like a pair of miscreant kids.

'I should have known! You pair of idiots!'

We looked at each other.

'You couldn't have made much more of a mess of this assignment if you'd tried. God knows what long-term psychological damage you've caused to those robots.'

I frowned, genuinely confused - after all we are just talking about a couple of machines here, however sophisticated.

'How did you know what was happening?' said Mike. 'You and your bunch of goons appeared like you've been spying on us all along.'

'Of course I knew what was happening. Do you think I'd let you two loose with the two most advanced robots in the world without constantly monitoring your every stupid, absurd, ill-considered action?'

'You mean - '

'Yes, you were being recorded every second you've spent in this house. There are cameras in every room that have captured your every brainless move.'

'Oh shoot, ' said Mike, recalling one or two incidents in particular, not necessarily involving the fleckers.

'That's illegal,' I said sternly, trying to recover some faint trace of credibility. 'You can't do that without our prior knowledge and written permission. It's a direct contravention of our legal and human - '

'So sue me,' replied Dr Smith.

'Even the toilet?' said Mike.

Natalie Smith paused.

'No, not the toilet.'

'I hope you ain't kidding. I ate one burrito too many jus' the night before last, an' I'm telling ya, the filling was just about enough to - '

Dr Smith summoned an impressive look of combined disgust and exasperation.

'I said not the toilet.'

Meanwhile the security detail had carried the now deactivated robots down the stairs and into a waiting van.

'Still,' said Dr Smith, 'I suppose if this fiasco has proved one thing, it's that humanity still has some way to go before it can prove itself worthy and capable of coexisting with robots on equal terms.'

'I - ', said Mike, and I covered him with a similarly insightful remark.

And with that Dr Smith gave us one last hard glare, shook her head and cleared out of the house with her security team. Leaving us to sit down at the kitchen table with a couple of cold beers from the refrigerator.

And at this point I think Mike, running a large hand ruminatively over his sweating face, expressed himself on behalf of us both with a true philosopher's detachment.

'Oh well,' he said, then took a large draught of beer and belched loudly.

Which Slice of Bread

I always have a terrible time trying to decide which slice of bread to take out of the packet which I habitually store in the fridge. I don't eat a lot of bread, so it can stay in there for well over a week, maybe ten days or more, sometimes even as much as a fortnight. I've never officially noted when I put a fresh loaf into the fridge - when I say fresh, I mean new, as in newly bought, but usually a cheap or budget large white sliced loaf, nothing fancy. That's something I really need to do at some point. But the main difficulty in choosing a particular slice, or rather more often pair of slices in the case of a sandwich, is the variation in thickness of each slice, which can be considerable. Of course there's other factors with bread that's been hanging around for a while, such as discolouration - patches of grey where it should be white. And sometimes the first signs of disintegration as pieces - often but not exclusively crusts - begin to detach themselves from the slice. But the sometimes extreme variation in width remains the major issue, certainly with the loaves I buy.

You would think in this day and age that all problems surrounding the production of bread would have been ironed out. But that is clearly not the case. Failures of quality control, lack of commitment at management level, poor or aging machinery, ill-conceived or indeed completely absent production protocols, a disillusioned workforce - wherever the blame lies - in some or all of the above, or some combination of the above in addition to other, unspoken, negative factors, the fact remains that much is still to be achieved in terms of research and development in the arena of bread production.

Every Last Stone or Pebble

Everything - every last stone or pebble - is kept exactly the same from year to year, century to century. Everything was catalogued and photographed long ago, and is rephotographed, remeasured, redocumented, and re-catalogued on a continuous basis. We are determined to keep everything as it was and has always been, into an indefinite future. Absolute stability is the basis and bedrock of our society. At the end of each month, when all documentation has been submitted confirming that all checks have been completed, all databases sifted, all records minutely examined and all evidence, including photographic, gone through with meticulous attention, to ensure that every building, road, wall, fence, tree, field, bush, flower, down to the smallest stone on wayside lane or pebble on the beach, is exactly as it was down to the smallest detail, and in precisely the same position as before - then the golden flags of compliance, continuity and conformity are hoisted on every hilltop and every high point. And in all the market squares golden horns are blown, and there is much rejoicing!

Why Do You Appear to be Inert?

I would like firstly to ask you why you allow your followers, adherents, disciples, call them what you will, to treat you as if you were a deity? The red carpet, the flowers strewn in your path, the weeping and wailing in ecstasy at your long-awaited arrival, the sinking to the knees in paroxysms of joy, the uplifted, expectant faces, docile, dog-like, practically mindless, having ceded all intellectual autonomy to their leader, master, messiah, redeemer, hero-in-chief.

From what I have learned of your philosophy - though you set no store by a discipline you describe as playing with shadows - nevertheless, from what I have learned, this trance-like hanging on your every word is directly antithetical to the meaning expressed in your teachings (though you claim not to be a teacher) on the subject of obedience. Which tells us that followers should not follow, that they should have the courage to be disobedient, to be their own master, obedient only to themselves. Yet at the same time you openly seek to deprogram them, to strip them of their minds, so that they are then free - free, that is, of will - to follow your teachings. A paradox which can surely only fill you with contempt for your slavish acolytes. Or is it their failure to appreciate the paradox that makes you privately spill over with disdainful laughter, even as you eat food lovingly prepared for you, sleep in sheets washed and ironed for you, in a bed made for you, and play with young women who freely (again a relative term in this context) offer themselves to you? Yet despite your private contempt, you manage invariably to present a benign, even beatific love for these poor dupes, both individually - if the word has meaning here - and collectively, an all-purpose all-enveloping blanket of warmth, tenderness and duplicity.

You say there is only the individual - no creed, no belief, no philosophy, no society, no religion, no God - nothing but the individual alone throughout their passage from cradle to grave. Yet to these people, deny it though you may, you *are* their God. They have ceased to be individuals in their own right. You have become their mind, their soul, their everything, their all. The only I in their lives is you.

But coming to the question that really interests me, why do you appear to be inert? I see you make no sign, nor utter any word in reply. Then let us continue. You decry ambition. You say that Life is its own goal. That all ambition and achievement is merely the projection of the ego. Yet without ambition there would have been no industrial revolution, no progress, no development - we would still be living a medieval subsistence existence. You might have been following the oxen at this very moment. You certainly wouldn't have that huge, and if I may say, ostentatious watch on your wrist. You wouldn't have that gleaming limousine parked outside waiting to take you wherever you want to go. No luxurious shower room. No hot water on tap. And so on - I don't want to labour the point.

Perhaps if we all still lived in dark age low-tech communities you would be active, physically healthy. As it is, you appear to be completely inert, a parasite living off - feeding off - the skills and hard work of your followers. Even your face is immobile, and your eyes have no expression. Does your silence imply agreement, dissension, or simply anger? Or, more appropriately, I suppose, complete disengagement?

Nales Place

That's Nales Place, that is. Which one? That one halfway up the hillside. You can't miss it. I can't see it. It's the big house. You can't almost see it with the trees in-between. You can see it in winter, though. It's about halfway up. I an't never been that far, to my knowledge, since I was a little un. I've been once. Long ago. It's a fair old walk up there. Quicker by motor o' course. It's a narrow lane. They keep a motor. Do they? They do. It's only a little tiny thing, but I've seen them in it, going up and down. Into the town and down to the beach. Not often, but I've seen them. I've never seen them, to my knowledge. They've a daughter. I've heard that. I've seen her. In the motor. You couldn't hardly see her, all huddled up in the back, but I seen her. Just a young thing, an't she? I couldn't hardly tell, all hunched up in the back of the motor. So I've heard. I've heard they don't get on. I haven't heard that. I've heard they're short o' money, 'n' may be movin' out soon. What does he do? Summat to do wi' films. Or so I've heard. Actor? Maybe. What else do you need in films? Someone to run the cameras. Aye, that's right, someone to run the cameras. What else would you need? Someone to make the scenery, maybe? That's true. Though there's plenty of scenery round here, what with the hills and the sea. They wouldn't want that though. I wouldn't know what they'd want. I've never been, nor wanted to. Nor I. It's summat for the young folk. Too much free time, that's their problem. That's true. They don't know the meaning of hard work, the young uns. Any road, that's Nales Place, that is.

The Music Teacher

She fell and couldn't get up again. She was soon over the shock of the fall, and then came the realization that her legs were numb and weren't responding. Quickly she rationalized the situation by telling herself it was just temporary paralysis, and in half an hour or so, an hour tops, she'd be fine and able to get up and go and put the kettle on. Meanwhile trying to work out how it had happened in the first place. One moment she'd risen slowly from her armchair, thinking a cup of tea would be nice for when the snooker resumed after the fifteen minute break. And the next thing she knew she was flat on her face, catching her head on something on the way down, and landing painfully on her right hip. She'd managed to turn herself over onto her back, bruised and shaken, and that was how things stood, or rather didn't.

In her youth she'd been tall, thin, shy, studious. Her emotional outlet had always been music. She loved with reckless passion Chopin and Brahms, Rachmaninoff and Liszt, Schumann and Greig, the super-romantics, and in moments of weakness, carried away by the music, she would imagine herself beautiful and glamorous, attended by handsome, eligible gentlemen entranced by her talent. Instead, retired from a lifetime of guiding the hot, grubby fingers of (mainly) small children through simple pieces while sometimes (often) needing to remind them which keys were which, a fledgling career as a virtuoso, her original ambition, necessarily abandoned due to lacking those last few percentage points of talent in favour of the day in, day out grind of teaching - instead, fate found her lying on her back on the carpet where she'd fallen, looking up at the ceiling and the crack she'd never noticed before.

The longer she looked at the crack - which extended almost the whole distance from the fireplace to the opposite wall - the more she wondered (wondering simultaneously at the illogic of her reflections, and whether they were symptoms of the blow to the head she'd received in falling) if it had some significance, carried some meaning for her life and the trajectory of her existence. She couldn't believe she'd never seen it before - but then she'd never been in this position before. It was like a timeline, with subtle indications along its length of events in her life which she'd almost forgotten. Had it always been there and grown as the years passed, with each deviation to left and right representing her fortune during that time, good and bad, things she had done, and things she had left undone? A comical enough idea, no doubt - a crack in the ceiling some kind of analogue to the painting of Dorian Gray. Most amusing. But in any case if it were truly equivalent would she not still possess the unblemished looks of her youth? What looks. There never were any looks to speak of, her looks at best equivalent to that spidery line across the ceiling. And there never were any suitors. She lay back and closed her eyes for several minutes. Her hip still ached painfully, and her head was throbbing. And there was still no response from her legs after several exploratory attempts. No-one ever called on her - she had no children, no close relatives, no friends. No-one would know what had happened if she couldn't reach her phone, which she'd left on charge in the bedroom.

She opened her eyes, drawn once more to the crack. Yes, a ridiculous, insane thought, to read meaning into its random meanderings. And yet. And yet there, near where the crack begins, close to the chimney breast, there, clearly, was where she fell off her bike and sprained her wrist when she was six. And there's where her glasses were broken when she was thirteen, when that fat girl at school had snatched them off her face and sat on them. She'd had to tell her parents they'd fallen off and she'd accidentally stepped on them. There was the death of her parents, unmistakeably so, two distinct deviations. And there (with a grimace of pain unconnected with her hip), that big wobble in the line, was where she gave up performing. Then a long, almost straight section, with hardly any divergences, indicating the long years of toil and loneliness. And there - there, near the end of the crack, close to the wall, it becomes so faint it's difficult to make it out. It seems to just fade away into nothingness. Even as dusk begins to fall outside the uncurtained windows, and the only light that touches the face of the music teacher comes from the streetlight across the road.

The World Awoke

The world awoke. The sun was shining. No doubt on that score. But not only was it shining, but shining brightly, merrily, even. And the clouds in the sky were gentle, fluffy and also neatly, artistically arranged. The tiger, normally at this time of day engaged in sharpening its ravening claws in preparation for the day's business, instead was smiling, as best a tiger, with that fearsome arrangement of teeth and jaws can smile, at some caterpillar proceeding slowly across a large leaf.

Spiders everywhere were carefully folding up their webs. If there was among them a hint of regretful nostalgia in this folding, it was well-concealed. One appeared to be observing a large fly creeping fitfully northwards along a blade of grass. As if contemplating how nourishing, tasty, even, it might be, if seasoned, salted, and served with a rich sauce. Before hastily dismissing this atavistic speculation.

'An evil huckster who wouldn't know the truth if it jumped out of the bushes with a fright mask on.'

'Yes, and what's more - '

'And to think those poor bastards somehow managed to miss out on the evolutionary process. Almost makes you feel sorry for them.'

'Almost. And you're right about - '

'Yes, almost.'

'She had this habit of laughing loudly and somewhat manically, then stopping abruptly, her face turned grim and rigid.'
'So what did you do.'
'What could I do? What could anyone do?'

'I'm interested in your opinion up to a point, but I disagree with it so fundamentally that I'm afraid I'm going to have to discount it and therefore ignore it.'

He didn't himself know where He had come from, which was a source of considerable disquiet and distress. He always claimed to be eternal, as that was the easiest way of resolving the problem, and everyone seemed to buy it. But on a rational level He couldn't quite bring Himself to believe it. It's true He never became older, but to Him, logically, that didn't necessarily signify that He had no beginning and no end. He had to dispense absolutes - He understood that. Any sign of ambiguity or doubt and they'd be on Him like a pack of wolves. If only they would understand that the claim to omniscience was a figure of speech.

'Even from when I was tiny and first began to crawl and move around, according to my mum I've been pretty much hyperactive ever since. I've never been diagnosed as such, so far as I know, but…'
'But what?'

'Just but.'

My friend Quorquoran would perform cart-wheels in the snow. 'Come on, young Liam! Follow my lead!'

'I wanna be part of it. I wanna be part of the whole God thing. Pick me for the team, God, willya? I don't wanna be on the subs bench, I wanna be on the team. Oh, pick me, God, pick me, willya? Willya? Say ya will! Oh say ya will!'

'You're going insane - and it's not a long journey.'

Thus soliloquised God. Along such lines as these, and for some time, God had been doing a bit of thinking.

'Not a lot, just a little,' cried one of the Archangels, laughing merrily, abusing his telepathic hotline, only to be crushed by a heavy-duty glare from the direction of the marble throne.

God cleared His throat, accompanied by another dark look.

'I think I've reached a decision.'
'Cool, dude.'
'Non-intervention can be taken too far.'
'Yeah.'
'Sure.'
'Absolutely.'

A bunch of young angels were hanging round the throne, hanging on God's every word, in fact.

'Ever played bridge?'
'Never been that keen on contact sports. I can think of better, more attractive ways of getting a concussion.'

'I don't feel well enough to work anymore. Not in the richest, fullest meaning of the word. I feel that ship has sailed upon the ocean of apathy and total disinterest.'
'You should take the afternoon off.'

'I'm humbled, privileged, honoured, over-whelmed, and pissed off. In that order.'
'That's interesting. On the other hand, popularity costs nothing except time, effort, and the inevitable compromise of one's inner unpleasantness. That's what I think, anyway. You may disagree. Not that that matters.'

'You see this is what I don't like about holistic medicine.'
'What?'
'The suggestion that the body knows what's good for it. It hasn't got a clue. It'll sabotage itself at the drop of a hat.'
'That's not what holistic means.'
'Well that's the inference.'
'Holistic means - '
'I don't care what it means.'
'Well you can't just invent meanings for words.'
'Can't I? Just watch me.'

'In a perfect world, nothing much would, or could, go wrong. Even if you wanted it to go wrong, whatever it was, it would refuse to do so. Or at least it would quietly intimate an unequivocal reluctance, in decided tones. A tart *niet*, I think not, perhaps.'

The angels exchanged knowing glances. This looked like being one of eternity's longer days.

'However - '

'Cool.'

'Lay it on me, dude.'

'That's good shit, man.'

'Silence!'

Betrayed by Myself

I was betrayed by myself. I turned myself in. Gave myself a ticket and a citation. Whispered incriminating testimony to the authorities. Ended up arresting myself. Gave myself an extralegal beating in my cell. Fabricated evidence against myself under self-inflicted duress. Paid witnesses to reveal the sordid truth about me in court. Bribed the judge to give me a longer sentence. And guess what, none of it worked. They found me not guilty and let me back on the streets, a menace to society, an ever-present danger to the public. It just doesn't make sense. But then what does.

The Unopened Parcels

Some call it a boxroom, some call it a study. Some even refer to it as a cupboard. Whichever way you look at it, it's not a huge room, and as you can see it's filling up quite nicely. Still, there's a little space left - just needs a quick game of parcel tetris. And I really need that space - I've just ordered the complete works (to date) of Stephen King, plus the complete works of William Shakespeare (poetry and plays) in a gorgeous leather-bound illustrated edition, as well as every book from the pen of Agatha Christie. Together, those books, inside their parcels, will take up possibly all of the remaining space. My ultimate ambition is to fill the room such that when someone opens the door they'll be faced with a solid wall of brown paper (plus stamps and labels), as smooth and flush as can possibly be achieved - a dense mass of parcelled books filling the entire space. And after that, who knows? There's the walk-in cupboard in my bedroom - or I could maybe even use the entire room. Or there's the kitchen, in which case I'd set up a portable cooker in the living room. The possibilities are literally infinite, and the sky is literally the limit.

Getting There

How am I doing? Well I guess that I'm doing fine. That is to say, not bad. Getting there, as they say. Wherever *there* is. That's the thing they never explain, the location of the *there* that we're all supposed to be getting to, or at least attempting to get to. And come to that, who is *they*? Who is the *they* who has (or have) come up with this absurd aphorism, but then never explains or elucidates? That's the question we should be asking - if in fact there's any point in asking any questions at all, when there are rarely if ever any satisfactory answers. Past the point of no return, as they say - that's another one. Again we have to ask, who is *they*? Who is the *they* who has/have made this pessimistic statement? Personally I prefer to believe that there *is* no point of no return, except in extreme instances. And extreme instances should never become the basis for inflexible axioms or aphorisms, as they say.

My Little One

Unearthly screaming from somewhere on the street outside. Unlike anything I've ever heard before. I refuse to go and take a look in case the movement of my curtains attracts the attention of whatever it is. Thoughts of what it is or might be fill my mind as I lie back down, rigid, staring at the ceiling. Thinking, I wish I could hear a car going past outside, or anything as proof of human activity - as a distraction, if nothing else. Then I hear a vehicle pass noisily over the stone setts as if summoned. Thankful for this, but only a temporary relief. At the same time my phone is flashing green, eerily lighting up the pile of DVDs on the small table next to my bed, indicating someone messaging me. I refuse to respond, or even look at the message at this time of night. Movement from above. Wondering, illogically, if there's some connection between the message on my phone and the screaming outside, which mercifully seems to have subsided, for now at least. Now footsteps above, creaking floorboards.

 Thinking back a few days to when I asked my daughter-in-law Natalie when she was going to pick up her little one, just two years old. She looked at me coldly, with a grim, sardonic half-smile and kept walking. When she came back into the room I asked the question again, When are you going to collect the little one? I received the same response. But this time, with a shock of realization, I said, Are you leaving her there overnight? I couldn't believe it, still can't believe it, even knowing what she's like, that she could be so cold, callous and uncaring. What does she know about the people she's leaving her child with? What will the little one be thinking, all alone in the night among people totally strange to her? Such coldness shocked and disturbed me to such an extent that I decided to go to the house of her captors, or jailers, call them what you will, and release my little one, take her away with me, come what may.

But when I got there I couldn't tell if it was her, Natalie's, house, or my house, or the house I sought - for in the dead of night they all looked alike, from the outside at least. And after parking my car I discovered there were now security guards on the door, black-clad, helmeted, menacing. They refused to speak when I demanded entry, but only looked at me with impenetrable coldness from under the rim of their helmets. Frustrated, I returned to the carpark, only to find my car missing, removed or stolen by somebody.

I can't think of anything now but my little one, left among strangers far away from home. I make my way to my daughter's house, but this too now has the same grim, black-clad security staff everywhere, precluding entry. Through the lit windows I can see that the place is overrun by strangers. Then from somewhere in the distance comes once more the unearthly screaming. Galvanised by fear, I play a cunning stratagem against the security guards, setting off a series of bangs which distract them sufficiently that, running swiftly into the shadows, I am able to find a half-open window, and climb through it into the house.

The first thing I discover is that my phone is missing. So now I am trapped in the house among complete strangers, unable to contact anyone, and with no means of escape. And with no-one there I know, including, apparently, my daughter-in-law, of whom there is no sign. And still all I can think of is my darling little one, abandoned among strangers, possibly at this very moment wide awake in total darkness, her eyes large and round in abject fear, gazing, sobbing, into the unfathomable nothingness. And meanwhile I am trapped here among strangers, my car and phone missing or appropriated, and with the unearthly screaming now louder than ever, and seemingly coming closer with every moment.

Chance Encounter

I met myself out walking one morning (an encounter as unexpected as it was tense). What are you doing out this early? Why should I not be out at this hour? That's a question you should be asking yourself. A question surely you also should be seeking to at least acknowledge, and if you can, refute. I fully intend to do both, and to my full satisfaction, but at a later date, when the general situation has calmed down somewhat and the barrage of recriminations has subsided. This whole affair is exceedingly unfortunate. Yet entirely unforeseen that matters should have so quickly reached a head. I would have said entirely predictable. Unfortunate and unforeseen. There I would disagree. With all due respect to your position, your recent intervention, far from defusing the situation, has merely further inflamed an already desperate state of affairs. An unwarranted and grossly exaggerated characterisation. I could easily make the same observation, and in precisely the same degree, regarding your recent comments, which I thought were particularly ill-judged, given the volatility and animosity between the two sides. You're employing a double standard - the instances you posit are in no way comparable. I believe them to be so. Nevertheless, I believe that your behaviour in this matter should be held to account. As should yours. You may as well know that

I shall be submitting a report to the proper authorities. As shall I. A full report. Make no mistake, mine shall be comprehensive. I may be consulting my solicitor. I shall certainly be in touch with mine at the earliest opportunity. We have nothing more to discuss. Very well. In that case I shall wish you a good day. Enjoy your walk. Enjoy yours.

Fwuck

No, I never use that unpleasant term. It's quite unnecessary. I always say fwuck instead. What? No, nobody notices a thing. I can say, for example, Fwuck off, you little fwucker, or Fwuck you, fwuckhead, and they'll just turn around and say, Beg your pardon, what did you say? - I didn't quite catch what you said. What do I say in reply? Oh, something like, I'm sorry, I'm struggling with a head cold. I was just asking, How are you doing? How's the wife? So you see I get all the satisfaction and emotional release of expressing my true feelings, but without actually offending anybody. Fwuck off, you fwucking fwuckhead, or I'll fwucking well fwuck you up, you fwucking little fwucker. It's really quite remarkably effective, and absolutely risk-free.

The Plague of Beards

'Next item on the agenda.'

They all looked at each other, knowing full well what was coming, indeed what they'd all been waiting for.

'Facial hair,' said the secretary dispassionately, and with a determinedly noncommittal expression.

Out of the blue there had been a sudden explosion of beards in the town. Such a pleasant, typical little English industrial town, it was the very last thing anyone expected. And yet perhaps not so unexpected.

A large number of young men from the town - larger than the national average - had been killed in the war. Women had taken over many of the roles within the town's mills and factories, and had refused to give them up after the war finished and men began to be demobbed and return to the town.

Supported by the local community, women had been voted in as town councillors, gradually displacing men, until eventually the entire council was comprised of women, including the positions of Mayor and 'Lady Mayoress'. Even the town clerk was a woman. And this all-female council now ran the town according to self-declared 'feminine principles'.

Of course, the feminisation of society - the ethos of caring, cooperation and emotional responsiveness - hadn't been embraced by everyone. There were dissenting voices - almost all men. Or as the Mayor called them, so-called men.

One of the by-laws passed recently by the council was that banning facial hair. Beards, moustaches, even sideburns beyond a prescribed maximum length, were all strictly prohibited as overt displays of undesirable masculinity. And that was when the problems really began.

Phoebe Lockwood was fifteen. Her mother was Mayor of Moreston. Feeling bored at home, both her mother and sister absent on business, Phoebe decided to follow into town. She got her bike out from the garage and set off down the narrow lane, losing herself in the magically mindless sensation of riding in the perfumed air, trees in full leaf lining the hedges, only occasionally having to negotiate a farm cart laden with hay, even more rarely a motor car.

She reached the outskirts of town, the road following the canal for a few hundred yards, then over the railway bridge. When she thought of Moreston objectively at all, she vaguely disliked it, though so used to it that she hardly gave it a thought - it was just there. The mills and factories with chimneys pouring out black smoke, streets of stone terraces, ponderous public buildings, cinemas, shops, everything soot encrusted, the air itself tangibly acrid, almost distinct enough to taste. She took a particular perverse pleasure in cycling past the gasworks with its unmistakable sweetish/rotten eggs smell.

Knowing her mother would be busy at a council meeting, Phoebe decided to head directly to Sunrise Mill, of which her sister Amelia was owner and managing director. But Amelia was busy with a broken-down machine and shooed her out. So Pheobe cycled a circuit around streets familiar to her in her forays into Moreston, and found herself in the only 'smart' part of town. Wherein resided Ambrose and Neville, both artists and aesthetes, and both with private incomes, who lived in adjoining bungalows, called Glencoe and Tintagel respectively.

They were both suitors for the hand of the beautiful and entrancing (Phoebe wouldn't have recognised this description of her sister) owner of one of the several woollen and worsted mills in Moreston, Amelia Lockwood. They competed with each other for her attention in letters and speeches of great sensitivity and emotionalism, to their target's considerable amusement.

About to pass the residence of Ambrose Smith, she saw him in the front garden up a ladder, pipe in mouth, trimming the hedge, and she waved. Ambrose, seeing Phoebe, somehow negotiated removing the pipe from his mouth while still holding the shears and without falling off the ladder, waved his hand still holding the pipe and called out to her.

'Phoebe!'

She pulled into the curb.

'Hello, Mr Smith.'

'Please, Ambrose.'

He came down the ladder, Phoebe observing with interest that his tall thin frame somewhat resembled the ladder, and came and stood beside her, smiling and peering through his spectacles.

'Out for a ride on your bicycle?'

'Yes, Mr Smith, I mean Ambrose.'

'That's good, that's nice. It's a beautiful day.'

'It certainly is.'

'I was just in the process of trimming my hedges.'

'Yes, I saw you.'

'Ah. So how are the summer holidays going? Looking forward to going back to school?'

'Okay, I suppose, and not really.'

'Ah. I share your reluctance. My own schooldays were…'

He seemed to hesitate for a moment over whether to reveal the true nature of his schooldays, but then decided to draw a veil.

'Oh, but I'm neglecting you! Can I offer you something to eat, a cake perhaps, and a glass of lemonade? You must be thirsty after all your activity.'

'Just the lemonade would be lovely, thanks.'

And just as Ambrose disappeared back into Glencoe, and reminding Phoebe of those little Black Forest weather houses where the figures pop in and out alternately, out popped Neville Cardew.

'Phoebe! How are you?'

Neville was a little shorter than Ambrose, with nice blonde hair, brilliantined and immaculately combed back.

'Very well, thank you, Neville, I mean Mr Cardew.'

'Please, Neville. So you're out for a ride on your bicycle?'

'Yes, Mr Car - , I mean Neville.'

Neville looked round, then leaned a little closer and dropped his voice.

'I wonder if you could do me a small favour?'

'Yes, of course, if I can.'

'I have this letter which - '

At this moment Ambrose returned with a glass of lemonade, casting a suspicious glance at Neville, who hastily returned the letter to his trouser pocket.

'Morning, Ambrose,' said Neville, in a toneless voice.

'Good morning, Neville,' equally toneless in response. 'Here's your lemonade, Phoebe,' handing her the glass.

'Thanks very much.' It had been a warm ride, and she drank it gratefully.

'I was just wondering - ' began Ambrose.

'So was I,' interrupted Neville. 'In fact just this moment I had asked Phoebe if she might - '

'What? What did you ask her?'

'With respect, that need not concern you. It's a private matter.'

'Oh don't be shy,' said Ambrose, with a grim smile. 'We are among friends.'

'Oh very well. I was about to ask Phoebe if she wouldn't mind delivering a letter.'

'Yes, of course,' said Phoebe. 'Who is it to?'

'Yes,' said Ambrose, 'who is it to?'

'Really, is that any of your business?'

'It might be.'

'It's really no problem,' said Phoebe, trying to placate the parties. 'I just need to know who to give the letter to.'

'Yes,' said Ambrose. 'Exactly. That's the key question.'

'Very well,' said Neville, once more pulling the letter from his trouser pocket. 'Would you mind, Phoebe, if it's at all convenient, giving this letter to your sister next time you see her?'

'Oh, so that's your game, is it.' Ambrose withdrew a letter from his trouser pocket. 'I was just about to ask, Phoebe, if it is at all convenient, whether you would mind delivering *this* letter to your charming sister, Amelia?'

'Oh really,' said Neville, with a look of utter disgust.

'Yes, of course,' said Phoebe hastily, 'I'll deliver both letters to Amelia as soon as I see her.'

A cascade of thanks followed, competing furiously with each other for fervency, followed by the letters themselves, in pink (Neville) and lavender (Ambrose) scented envelopes.

'Be very sure that you deliver my letter, won't you, Phoebe,' said Ambrose anxiously.

'Don't worry Mr...Ambrose, I will.'

Phoebe put the letters in the basket of her bike.

'Oh do be sure that *my* letter doesn't blow away, Phoebe,' cried Neville.

'Don't worry, I'll be careful.'

And with a cheery wave she set off once more, leaving the two contestants standing side by side on the pavement gazing anxiously after her.

She thought of going back to the mill to deliver the letters, but having just been unceremoniously chased away, decided that Amelia would have to wait till she got home.

'The question is, what is to be done.'

'It's just childish. Ridiculous.'

'It's worse than that. It's emblematic. Or symptomatic. One of the two.'

'Of what?'

'Resentment, of course. They've resented us for years, and everything we've achieved.'

'I said all along the by-law was unnecessary and provocative. But nobody would listen. And now we're faced with this reaction. This was all completely avoidable. All there ever was were a few moustaches here and there, not doing any real harm to anyone. And never a beard in sight. And now look where we are - inundated, beards everywhere, right, left and centre.'

'I don't remember you saying anything of the kind.'

'We cannot allow this situation to continue.' The Mayor, Mrs Marjorie Lockwood, in full regalia and with magisterial presence and commanding voice had spoken, and everybody fell, momentarily at least, silent. 'We have to nip this in the bud before it gets out of hand, using any and every means at our disposal. We have not worked all these years in pursuit of such lofty goals, only to be implicitly taunted by a few so-called men.'

'More than a few,' piped up Miss Ancroft, small and fiery. 'Anyway I know what I'd like to do to them.'

'It's outright defiance.'

'It's only a by-law, when all's said and done. We shouldn't make too much of this.'

'Nevertheless,' continued the Mayor. 'Even by-laws must be respected and enforced. Otherwise the whole system of local government to which we are dedicated would simply disintegrate. No, we must regard this as a litmus test for our whole movement. All of these beards that have suddenly sprung up, large and small, *must go*! There can be no exceptions!'

'But how? How can we enforce it? Without the support of the community our hands are tied.'

'Who says we don't have the support of the community,' said Miss Ancroft angrily.

'Who says we do?'

'Me!'

'Could we try persuasion?' suggested Mrs Taylor, a good-humoured moderate, relatively speaking.

'Out of the question.'

'Well, what about buying them off?'

'Buying them off?'

'What if we were to pay all the beard wearers say five pounds, or even two or three pounds, to shave off their beards and remain clean-shaven for at least a year. I think most if not all would jump at the offer.'

'We need armed patrols.'

'Oh for goodness sake.'

'Well we need to do something, and soon, or else we'll be faced with an epidemic.'

'Buying them off,' said the Mayor, 'sounds very much like giving in to blackmail. Besides, once it became public knowledge that the council was giving five pounds away to anyone wearing a beard, we'd suddenly see beards sprouting everywhere. Even some women might be tempted to see if they could qualify; some, I believe,' looking round at the members of the council, and making a mental note of those who failed to meet her eye, 'might even succeed. No, it's out of the question. As for the other suggestion regarding patrols - not to mention some form of sanction - I think it expedient at this moment to rule nothing out.'

Rather than going straight home, Phoebe continued past the family mansion and further up the lane towards where the Hall stood, almost hidden within extensive grounds, shielded by a screen of mature trees and a high wall around its perimeter. The house was the seat of Sir Morlac Thorsden, a shadowy figure rarely seen outside his grounds, but often given to writing splenetic letters to the local press castigating what he described as the 'sentimentalised, feminised direction of society', which would inevitably lead to a 'complete breakdown, as men rose up to reclaim their immemorial rights'. Phoebe had always secretly thought the house likely to be a hotbed of ghouls and other supernatural creatures, probably including the mysterious Sir Morlac himself.

She pulled up outside the lodge house and peered through the gates. The lodge itself appeared deserted, and the main house was hidden from view. Quite abruptly both gates began to swing slowly open. Startled, Phoebe looked for some mechanism that could account for the movement, but could see none. Curiosity winning out over fear, she began to cycle cautiously up the drive, seemingly drawn to the house against her will.

It came into view at last, a rambling Tudor mansion of several stories, in a state of some disrepair. She parked her bike, walked up to the main door, then saw her hand take hold of the heavy knocker. The sound of three loud knocks could be heard reverberating through the old house, as if it were completely empty. But just as with the lodge gates, the door swung slowly open, and Phoebe found herself in a hallway lit only by candles, filled with gloomy portraits, flags, shields and swords displayed upon the walls and on the staircase ahead of her.

She jumped as a tall figure appeared without warning at her side, and found herself looking up into the longest, queerest face she had ever seen. It even seemed to have some kind of strange twist to it. The face had a very long, thin nose, neatly trimmed dark beard, and equally dark hair swept back from a high forehead. Darkest of all were the eyes, black as night. Phoebe couldn't decide how old this apparition was - simultaneously youthful, yet also very old. For some reason she didn't feel afraid.

'Well hello, my young friend.' The voice was deep and sonorous and, on the face of it, friendly. 'Thank you for dropping in. I get so few visitors. I am Sir Morlac Thorsden. And you, I take it, are the Mayor's daughter.'

'Yes, that's right. My name's Phoebe Lockwood. And…and this must be your house.'

She didn't wonder at the time how he knew who she was. She was too fascinated by his strange, uncanny face, and those deep, dark eyes and that most melodious voice. And the house she had long wished to explore.

'Yes, let me show you around. I'm afraid it will all seem a little old-fashioned to your young eyes.'

It was as if he knew what it was she desired above all else. And it was all quite wonderful to Phoebe, despite or perhaps because many parts of the building seemed full of shadows, half-forgotten and even semi-derelict in places. They made their way from the library, lined with musty, decaying volumes, to the Great Hall, then morning room, chapel, banqueting hall, through all kinds of narrow connecting passageways and twisting stairways. She'd lost all sense of where she was in the building when they arrived in the long gallery, directly overlooking acres of neglected parkland.

And as they walked along the gallery, once more lined with portraits, Phoebe asked if they were all his ancestors. Her companion laughed.

'No indeed! In fact, I bought this property nearly thirty years ago, and have changed nothing. It was and is perfectly suited to my taste. These people,' waving his hand at the portraits, 'are members of the family that owned the house continuously for the four hundred years or so before my time. They are now like old friends, and I take comfort from having them around me. They give me a sense, or illusion, of family,' smiling sadly.

When at last they returned to the library, Sir Morlac offered Phoebe refreshment, which she declined, saying she'd really better be getting home. He saw her to the door.

'Pass on my kind regards to your mother, if you would, Phoebe.'

'Yes, I will, of course. Do you know her?'

'Our paths have crossed,' he replied, with a strange smile from that queer, twisted face.

Marjorie Lockwood looked askance at her daughter.

'You've been to the Hall?'

'Yes, I just…dropped in.'

'You dropped in?' Her mother's voice pitched unusually high and with an incredulous, almost frantic tone.

Phoebe couldn't remember now how or why she'd found herself inside the Hall, or even how she'd got back home. Presumably she'd cycled, but she couldn't remember doing so. It was like a dream where you can recall only a few disconnected fragments.

'I found myself there, and then Sir Morlac showed me over the Hall.'

'I can't believe that you would be so foolish as to put yourself in that position.'

'Nothing bad happened. He seemed very kind, if a little strange.'

'Anything could have happened, my girl. Are you so naïve? Especially in the current climate.'

'He knew I was your daughter.'

'How did he know? Did you tell him?'

'No, he just seemed to know.'

Her mother looked thoughtful and concerned.

'It's almost like some kind of veiled threat,' she said quietly, as if to herself. 'You must be more careful in future, Phoebe.'

'Okay, I will.'

'I mean it. This Sir Morlac is our most vocal and vociferous critic and opponent. It's he who is stirring up this ridiculous rebellion, from the comfort of his stronghold. This...beard business.'

'I noticed quite a few men with beards as I cycled through town today. I thought it was rather odd - and funny.'

'It is far from funny. It is a very serious and deeply disturbing matter.'

'Oh okay.'

'And remember what I've told you.'

Phoebe found her sister in her room going over some accounts at her desk. She plonked herself down on the bed.

'Mummy seemed a bit worked up just now.'

'Mm. What about?'

'Oh, just political stuff, things going on in town. Beards mainly.'

'Oh not all that stuff again. It's all just a substitute, you know.'

'For what?'

'Oh you're far too young to understand.'

'For sex, you mean.'

Amelia turned round in her seat, her eyes wide, eyebrows arched, then laughed uproariously.

'Not so young then, I see,' she said at last.

'Has mummy never had a...'

'A male best friend or admirer? said Amelia, smiling. 'Not that I'm aware of.'

'Not in all the time since daddy died?'

Phoebe had been conceived in the last few months of the war when their father, an infantry major, had been on leave. He'd returned to France, only to be killed a couple of weeks before the Armistice. Phoebe's thoughts often turned to the father she had never met, wondering what kind of person he'd been, and what characteristics she'd inherited from him. Her mother never spoke of him, and Phoebe had long ago given up asking, though Amelia had shared a few memories from when she was young, and Phoebe took what she could from those.

'I don't think so. Nothing serious anyway. Ever since she got involved in politics and the whole women's movement thing - which I totally support, of course - I think that has fully absorbed her interest and energy.'

'So what about you, then?'

'What do you mean, what about me?'

'Well, are you also too fully absorbed, by the mill in your case, to have a - '

'You precocious brat!' Trying to convey some measure of indignation through her laughter.

'Oh well, maybe it's not too late. And on the same subject I've got these letters for you, one from Ambrose, and one from Neville. They're both scented, by the way,' ostentatiously sniffing each envelope in turn, then holding them out for Amelia, who snatched them from her hand.

'Now get out.'

'Is that all the thanks I get? You know, they were practically fighting over you earlier - I really can't think why.'

'I said get out!'

'Okay,' said Phoebe, smiling. 'Enjoy reading them, my dear and darling Amelia! I just can't stop thinking about you, and your beautiful - '

Amelia made a threatening gesture, at which Phoebe scampered from the room.

By now there were beards everywhere. It had become a veritable plague and public nuisance. Dogs cowered and hid under farm carts, cats hissed and arched their backs before shooting off at high speed. Children were routinely upset, tearfully refusing to play outside or go to bed without a light on. In short, something had to be done.

In seeking a solution, and as a preventive measure, the council instituted patrols. Two motorbike and sidecar combinations were purchased, and four hefty women hired as patrol officers, or beard wardens as they were known informally, wearing specially designed uniforms and helmets in pink to match the livery of the motorbike and sidecars. They toured the streets during daylight hours when beards were most visible and the nuisance therefore at its worst.

The work was heavy. Beards were omnipresent. The wardens were empowered to issue a ticket giving an offender fourteen days to either remove the beard, or face a ten pound fine. Some of those caught simply ran away, while some tore up the ticket and threw it in the face of the issuing officers, who without the power of arrest were hamstrung. The patrols quickly became a laughing stock.

An emergency council meeting was called. The patrols reported on their experiences, and it was agreed that another approach might be necessary. Miss Ancroft suggested mounting machine guns on the sidecars, but the Mayor pointed out that this was England, and whereas such tactics might be acceptable in Italy or Germany, it might not go down too well here.

One of the officers relayed the important news that they had seen a crowd begin to gather, and had heard a rumour that this rally of bearded men was to be addressed by Sir Morlac Thorsden. Anxious looks were exchanged, and council members wondered aloud in a babble of worried voices whether this could signal an uprising.

'This is all so unfair, and so typical,' began the Mayor, quieting the din. 'Everything's been so much better, more peaceful and fairer since women took charge. We've created a new atmosphere and ethos in the town. And not just for women, but also men. The opportunities we've created for women to meet socially, nursery provision, kiddies clothing for those who can't afford it, extra support for the unemployed, opportunities for women to meet socially, and get an education through evening classes. Moreston has been a better, nicer place since women have been running it. And men just can't take it. They so hate the fact of women being in charge. So-called men,' bitterness in her voice and heart, 'who have had it all their own way since time began.'

'I still say we should fit machine guns to the sidecars.'

Phoebe had cycled into town to meet a friend and go to the cinema. On turning a corner by some shops she saw just ahead, on the green by the church, a large crowd of bearded men. She had never seen so many beards gathered in one place. She rode as close as she dared, then paused and dismounted, suddenly realising that the figure on the platform orating passionately was none other than Sir Morlac Thorsden. She pushed her bike around the side of the gathering to get a better view of the platform. There was something about his voice that both transcended meaning and commanded attention. It hardly seemed to matter what words came out of his mouth, the sound and passion alone were enough to convince and delight his audience.

Phoebe began to be feel carried away herself, held in the spell of his voice. For some reason she imagined the spittle flying from his mouth in the intensity of his emotion, first coating his beard, then flowing from his beard to the ground, becoming a torrent that enveloped his audience, before starting to flow down the streets, swelling with greater and greater force until the entire town was engulfed, and people climbed to upper stories of buildings, and some even onto roofs to try to escape the flood. The inhabitants could gauge the force and level of his emotion by the level of the torrent. Markers were set into walls to show levels that had previously been reached. From this data mathematicians were able to -

She came back to herself just as the speech was ending in a grand peroration, Sir Morlac calling for an end to male oppression, an end to beard oppression, and the freedom for all men to wear a beard, without let or hindrance, which was after all nothing less than their birthright.

After whipping his audience into a semi-frenzy, he then brought them down to earth again with a call for calm, and a directive that there should be only peaceful protest, as they were civilized men and, above all, Englishmen. He promised to personally intervene with the council on behalf of all the men of Moreston on this most important issue and burning question. There followed a prolonged period of cheering, after which the crowd began slowly to disperse.

Sir Morlac spotted Phoebe at the edge of the crowd, and beckoned her over. He greeted her like an old friend, smiling and shaking her hand.

'Phoebe, how are you? What did you think of the speech?'

'It seemed to go over very well, from what I heard. I didn't know you were a public speaker.'

In fact she had no idea he went out in public at all.

'Well, one has these little hidden talents! To be serious for a moment, I have an apology to make. And a request.'

Phoebe looked at him inquiringly.

'I suppose you gathered that the purpose of this meeting, in relation to the wearing of beards, is very unfortunately in opposition to the dictates of the council, of which your mother, as Mayor, is of course the leader.'

'That's really nothing to do with me,' said Phoebe. 'I have no interest in politics.'

'Nevertheless, I should hate to be the means of causing you any anxiety or upset.'

'Don't worry at all, you aren't. I'm really not bothered.'

'Very well. Then to my request. I should very much appreciate an opportunity to meet with the members of the council to discuss this unfortunate matter directly. If you, Phoebe, were able to speak to your mother, informally, to see whether a meeting might be possible, I would be most grateful. I believe any direct approach by myself would be dismissed out of hand. But if you were able to intercede - you could perhaps say that I believe a compromise to be feasible - then possibly something might be done. Would you be able to do that for me, Phoebe?'

'Yes, of course, I'll certainly try. Though I don't know how my mother will take it.'

'That is all I ask. And thank you.'

Back home that evening, following a great deal of strenuous argument, Phoebe was finally able to persuade her mother to allow Sir Morlac to attend a council meeting. Mainly because both she and the council were completely out of ideas on how to solve this most pressing problem. Arrangements were hastily made for him to attend an emergency meeting the next day.

The members of the council waited nervously. There had been considerable heated opposition to the idea of the ringleader of their opponents attending the meeting, but the force of personality of the Mayor, as was customary, prevailed.

Sir Morlac Thorsden duly arrived - a beard in their midst! And for everyone there it was their first sight of him, this tall, singular figure, who greeted them all pleasantly and courteously, and was directed to a chair at the council table. There was some initial muttering and even some hissing from the direction of Miss Ancroft, though this was swiftly quieted by the Mayor. Daggers of hatred continued to fly across the room (courtesy of Miss Ancroft), and embed themselves in Sir Morlac who, however, appeared not to notice.

He quietly put forward a proposal similar to that previously mooted - compensation for the voluntary removal of beards, but also allowing those who wished to do so to retain their beards. Almost all the members of the council were, despite themselves, mesmerised by his voice, his eyes, and even his beard. The Mayor managed to rally and stay calm, and forwarded a counter proposal, agreeing to the concept of compensation for beard removal, dependent on remaining clean-shaven for at least a year, even though this proposal would be problematic from a financial viewpoint. But also (a spur of the moment inspiration) she proposed the appointment of a 'beard czar', a recognized aesthete who would have the final say on who, of those who wished to remain bearded, would be allowed to do so - a judgment to be made on purely aesthetic grounds - and even then a fifteen shillings annual fee would be payable.

After a few moments consideration, Sir Morlac agreed to this compromise, and further said that he would personally underwrite the financial cost of the compensation. This seemed to clinch the matter, and while Sir Morlac waited outside the council chamber a vote was taken, and the motion passed unanimously.

An aesthete was duly appointed. Tall, thin, severe, her hair cut short and wearing a monocle, she was part of the artistic circle of Ambrose and Neville who, scrupulously clean-shaven themselves, while declining to participate in any direct action, had volunteered their moral support. She was allocated a temporary office in the council building. In no time at all there appeared a queue of bearded men (some apparently only recently bearded), very much like a soup kitchen line, the vast majority of course there only to collect their five pounds. Only occasionally was the professional judgment of the aesthete required, and she duly and dispassionately made the appropriate decision in all cases.

So civil war was averted, thanks at least in part to the intercession of Phoebe Lockwood. Moreston settled back into the friendly, low-key little town huddling in the valley it had always been. As for Sir Morlac and Phoebe, they remained friends, and as she entered adulthood he encouraged her to reach for her dreams and strive to fulfil her full potential. And by the 1950s, twenty or so years later, whether this encouragement had had any tangible effect or not, or whether more inspired by the feminist movement in Moreston led by her mother, or simply due to her own persistence, Dr Phoebe Lockwood was a successful and respected academic and researcher, with an extensive publication record and a growing reputation.

Everything Simply Evaporates

I remember, I remember, I remember. What do you remember? I remember people, places, things, stolen moments, stolen chunks of jelly from the pantry, a spoonful of Bournvita sticking to my teeth (prelude to a long series of uncomfortable visits to the dentist in years to come), a ten shilling note found in my brother's room and secretly secreted, later to be spent on toys, guilt still reaching out decades later, endless days of play and sunshine, soil and grass, shady secret places, special toys, forgotten friends, half-remembered aunts and uncles like wind-up mannequins or marionettes, set in motion to perform their set routines, uncle's tricks, a florin suddenly appearing from my ear, auntie's round and pleasant though wizened face, cruelly mocked, then back into their box again till next time. What do you remember? I remember faces, shadows, reflections, fleeting reminiscences of days long past, long lost, which in reaching out to touch dissolve into mist. What do you remember? I remember everything, and everything I remember now is gone, but for the only thing worth learning or remembering, that everything simply evaporates, as if it had never been.

The Poet

There's nothing worse than being a misunderstood poet. Poets should always be correctly understood. That goes without saying. As for the poetry itself, that's a completely different matter. As I was saying to Stevie last night, That's a completely different kettle of fish. She said, What is? I didn't pursue it. I thought if she's determined to wilfully pretend not to understand me, or to not understand me - or to misunderstand me - that's her affair, I say that's her whistle and flute. Anyway, I thought, Stevie's not even your real name, so who are you to lecture me on semantics or etymology. We could all choose to change our names, we could all pretend to be someone else. But it doesn't do any good, and it doesn't change anything in the long run, I say it doesn't really alter the trajectory of your life in any meaningful way. I mean I could say my name is Edward, and then ask some half-forgotten poet if they think there's any mileage in having a q in Edward, as in Edqward, or I could call myself Zadie when my name's actually Sadie and hope that nobody notices, but it doesn't really do any good in the long run, I say that's your Lionel Ritchie. I put the matter to Wilfred, but he said q is never followed by w, only by u - everyone knows that. I didn't pursue it. Of course I knew that, but I thought if he's determined to be one of those remorseless grammar zealots then that's his problem, I say that's his Zippy and Bungle. As I was saying to Wystan just the other day, I said, Have you ever noticed how Noel Edmond's beard has developed over the years? I think it started midway through the run of Deal or No Deal. He turned his massive, disintegrating features away from me and towards the dying light, and modulated imperiously, I never pay attention to such matters. I thought, Alright darling, keep your hair on, I say mind your apples and oranges. Anyway, I didn't pursue it.

Making a Difference

I have come to the conclusion that everything around me exists solely for my amusement, and that my interest, or not, in what goes on determines what form those events and actions take, even down to the appearance and existence of the actors themselves. People tend to disappear when I lose interest in them, which leads me inevitably to infer that their existence is predicated entirely on my interest or regard for them. Of course, people always come and go, but this goes beyond mere coincidence.

For example - and there have been so many over the years that it's difficult to narrow it down to a few specific incidents - there was a young woman I regularly encountered at the bus stop. I couldn't decide at first if she was a boy or girl - not that it's of any consequence, to me or anyone else. Eventually I decided that, on balance, there was something more feminine than masculine in her behaviour and demeanour, though her tout ensemble continued to be decidedly androgynous. Somewhere between seventeen and nineteen was my estimation, probably in her final year at high school, or first or second year at college or university.

Tall, slim, dressed all in black - black jacket, loose black jeans, black Doc Martens. Her hair was cut very short, and there was a discreet tattoo of a crescent moon and a few stars on the back of her neck (I noticed this while sitting directly behind her on the bus as she flicked through photos of herself and friends on her mobile). Quiet, reserved in manner, invariably immersed in her phone, both while waiting at the bus stop and on the bus. So I had ample opportunity to study her looks, while still making it appear, as a precaution, that I'd just happened to look her way. And she had the most beautiful head and face - both full face and in profile - that I have ever seen. I rapidly became obsessed by her beauty, which to me seemed like something out of Greek mythology or some previously undiscovered creation of Michelangelo.

Then one morning as I was walking to the bus stop, I turned a corner and there she was a few yards in front of me, also on her way to catch the bus. And for the first time I noticed (that I had never noticed before) that she walked with a particularly ugly, ungainly gait, like a sailor on leave, or perhaps an agricultural labourer. Feeling cheated and betrayed, I could hardly bear to continue looking at her. And from that moment on the spell was broken, and I lost all interest in her. And very soon afterwards she stopped appearing at the bus stop - my sudden lack of interest had clearly had a decisive effect.

Then there was the case of an old man, round and squat, who suddenly began to appear, making his way to the bus stop in a singularly laboured fashion, bent forwards as if against an opposing force. He walked extremely slowly, but with maximum effort and determination, like a professional race walker, only with minimal progress. Head down, full concentration, puffing and blowing audibly as he eventually went past. I made the mistake one day - fascinated by the whole range and combination of his actions, from the little plump legs and tiny steps, to the piston-like arm movements, fists clenched, driving forwards, elbows jutting out on each backward stroke, to the pursed rictus of his mouth as he noisily exhaled - of looking at him rather too obviously and with too much particularity. Of course, once I realised he'd noticed me watching him, he lost interest for me as a subject of study. And almost immediately after that he disappeared as abruptly as he'd materialized in the first place - which was only to be expected.

These examples seem to be exclusively bus-related, so let's choose another category as evidence. People I intensely dislike - and for this to work I have to know them personally or to have had some personal contact with them - tend not to last very long once I concentrate my hatred upon them. I wouldn't go so far as to say I have the evil eye, but it would seem that something along those lines is happening. Once I focus my attention on somebody with feelings not merely of distaste or even active dislike, but real, deep, visceral loathing, they soon begin to go rapidly downhill - or even drop dead more or less straight away. It's a curious phenomenon, but has happened so many times now that I'm no longer surprised, merely gratified in a suitably malevolent and vindictive way.

After all, we all have our little whims, tics and fads, and none the worse for that. It all adds spice to existence, it adds texture and flavour, not to mention aroma, the sweet smell of vindication, providing solid proof that my existence has meaning and a tangible, almost measurable effect on the world. I like to think I'm, as they say, making a difference.

The Power Station

'There is nothing to suggest it's a living entity.'

'I believe it to be so.'

'But it's a man-made artefact.'

'That is not important. That is not a factor. In any case I dislike and object to the term "man-made". It is archaic and androcentric. It should never be used in any context in the modern world.'

'I accept your rebuke, and withdraw the term.'

'Apology accepted.'

'It was not an apology - in using that expression I had done nothing to you or against you personally that demanded an apology. It was simply an acknowledgement, on a purely intellectual level, that my use of the term, which I shall not repeat, was inappropriate. Therefore I withdraw it.'

'While I thank you for not repeating the term in question, I believe that your admission carried within it at least an implicit apology, in that the use of, in your own words, an inappropriate term, might well have caused me to suffer a certain level - impossible to quantify as it might be notwithstanding - a certain level of mental pain, approaching almost to the threshold of torture.'

'Such was not the case, was never the case, nor was it ever my intention. Besides which - '

'But to return to the matter at hand, I've heard from very good, very reliable sources that there is a plan in hand - more or less set in stone, or so I've heard - to decommission the station within two years.'

'I think not.'

'Your use of the terms "think" and "not" in conjunction are, I have to say, causing me a high level of stress, amounting almost to the threshold of trauma.'

'I apologise.'

'The term you have just uttered is, I've just decided, particularly offensive to me, and I demand that you withdraw it.'

'Then I withdraw it, with my…I withdraw it.'

'Too late. The use of the term "withdraw" is peculiarly offensive to me, and explicitly injurious to my mental health.'

'Then I withdraw my entire vocabulary, and with your explicit permission will proceed to insert any blunt object of your choice up your - '

'Your use of the term "proceed" followed, after a number of other words, by the terms "blunt", "object", "of", "your", "choice", "up", and "your", in this context and in conjunction, I find extremely offensive, and particularly injurious to my - '

'Good. They were meant to be.'

Buck

He's putrefying even as you look at him. He's alive (so they say, and it's true there's plenty of bulk to back that assertion), but he's already rotting. The stench of putrefaction follows him like a cloud of flies. That's Buck Brady. That's my boss. That's the Buck I know. Yes, Mr Brady, straight away. A businessman, of sorts (the worst sort), so temperamentally coarse that insults, no matter how personal or disgusting, roll straight off him like water off teflon. He regards abuse - the more offensive the better - as the normal and acceptable coin of social intercourse - the insults and name-calling just the sort of thing he would do himself, and does on a daily basis. Of course he wouldn't put it that way himself. Waddya say? Coina what? Waddya talkin about? Nothing Buck, I mean Mr Brady. I was just saying you're just the best, the best at makin' coin like there's no tomorrow, like nobody else. Never been nobody like me 'n this business. Best there's ever been, or ever will, nobody seen nuthin' like it before, 'n' prob'ly never will again. I got more properties on my books in this whole area than anyone's ever seen or ever will. You grotesque, ignorant, conceited clown. That's right, Mr Brady. Only one Buck Brady, an' a'm it. You sure are, Mr Brady. You big, stinking pile of horse manure. Buck Brady, Sales and Letting Agent, The World of Affordable Homes. Or the

World of Theft and Intimidation, as I call it. A world in which, to my shame, I'm intimately involved - but not for much longer.

He started off in auto restoration did Bucky boy, twenty or so years ago. As I heard it he'd pick up some old heap of junk, a classic in its day and just starting to shoot up in value. Then instead of a proper body or frame-off full strip-down restoration, he'd do a super quick botch job, a few rudimentary weld spots here and there, just enough to hold for a week or two (if you're lucky), plus gallons of filler, especially to plug gaping rust holes in structural members. Then a shiny, glossy respray to look a million dollars, just the thing to pull in the unwary, and then with any luck this rolling piece of garbage might actually make it fifty miles before something important collapsed or dropped off.

And taking the car back (on the end of a recovery truck) to air your grievances with Buck Brady, and maybe even demand a refund, wasn't something for the faint-hearted. For that matter, being in a small office with Bucky isn't for the faint-hearted, or anyone with a sense of smell, the bouquet a combination of rank body odor, bad breath, aftershave and decay, as if the very core of his body had begun to decompose, and the stench was coming up through his pores. He'd unwedge his giant butt from the chair where he was looking through receipts and invoices, grunting as he slowly turned his six foot, two hundred and fifty pound barrel of a body to face his unhappy customers, while from a large, round, podgy face, topped by thinning blonde hair, a pair of cold, hostile pig's eyes fastened on theirs. Nope, no sir Mr Brady, thank you for your custom, quality work only undertaken at our own Classic Car Restoration and Sales Center, bespoke restorations carried out by our skilled craftsmen and experienced engineers - no, only the very brave, foolhardy or fearless would face off with Bucky. And even then they'd never see a dime.

As far as the intimidation goes, it's a little different for me. For one thing, I've got a college education, Business & Management Studies degree, something that fat pile of excrement could never get within a million miles of. And for another, I'm six five and I work out, so while I'm wary of him I'm not scared of him. In fact he hired me for that very reason, my physical presence and its effect on tenants, either alongside him doing the rounds of his properties, me playing the part of bodyguard, or on my own chasing up late payers. But I'm getting ahead of myself. After a couple of years fleecing customers out of big dollars with his fake restoration business, he abruptly quit that, decamped with a sizeable pot of dough, and started buying up properties in the city. And now he owns around a hundred and fifty, so this is big business, a big operation. But big though it is, he likes to stay hands-on, making personal visits and phone calls if he thinks a tenant needs a quick reminder of who Buck Brady is and what he's capable of.

What kind of landlord is he? Just the worst kind, the worst of the worst. He packs people in like sardines, multiple families in one flat, multiple safety violations. Lucky for Bucky the laws don't apply to him, all those basic, standard laws protecting tenant rights. The properties in his portfolio are generally in a terrible state of repair. He buys cheap and doesn't spend a dime on improvements or maintenance. Holes in ceilings, wires trailing everywhere, mold and more mold, windows that won't open, heating that doesn't work, showers that don't work, torn or missing carpets. A thorough inventory of contents? Good one. Gas and electrical safety checks? Don't make me laugh. Hiking the rent halfway through the tenancy? Standard practice for Buck. Deposit protection? Yeah no. Entering the property uninvited and threatening or harassing tenants? Fair game for Buck Brady. Eviction without legal grounds? No problem for Bucky, because like I say the laws don't apply to him. How does he get away with it? Expensive lawyers and understandably reluctant witnesses. He doesn't care about any of it just so long as the money keeps rolling in, and that's the bottom line. If the property fell down, he'd still have the land value.

Anyway, this is where I'm supposed to come in. As there's unfortunately only one of him, and big though he is he can only spread himself so far, I'm his eyes and ears on the ground, constantly making the rounds of the properties, making unexpected, unscheduled visits, chasing up late payers, applying pressure. And God's truth is I just don't know how much longer I can keep it up. You've got to be able to live with yourself, and working for Buck Brady makes that difficult. Lately I've begun to play a dangerous game. Between ourselves, I've taken to cooking the books against Buck, going into the accounting records on the computer, somewhere Buck rarely goes - he's still in the age of bits of paper he can hold in his podgy hands, and burn when necessary - and change entries so it reads that those of Buck's tenants who are struggling the worst have paid their rents and are up to date, when in fact they may be months behind. Just to give them a breathing space and put off eviction a little longer. Of course it's only a matter of time before Buck or his crooked accountant catch on to what I've been doing. By which time I plan to be far, far away, and beyond the reach of Buck Brady (I hope).

The Unanswered Questions

I kept talking to him, I mean in terms of attempting to perpetuate a dying conversation, until at last he ceased to reply. He turned his head a few degrees, maybe as much as ten, from true. Then refused to speak. And never spoke again, so far as I know, though this remains to be definitively established. For myself, despite this setback, I continued occasionally to put what I considered particularly pertinent and searching questions to him, in the hope they might pique his interest and involuntarily force some kind of reply. And occasionally I did think I detected a flicker of interest, if not yet any sign pointing to the potential of full engagement - merely the suggestion of a smile, ironic or otherwise, again a slight turn of the head, though much less than formerly, perhaps even unnoticeable to the untrained eye.

I would sometimes ask quite involved rhetorical questions, of course expecting no reply, but hoping at least to engage his interest - prime him, in short, for my next question, whatever that might be, but certainly a direct question, practically demanding a response, hoping that the arcane convolutions of my preceding inquiry might, as I say, have sufficiently engaged his attention, elicited his interest, drawn him out of his torpor of disengagement, such as to actually compel some kind of reply, though of course without success.

Or sometimes I would take a quasi-prosecutorial approach: Mr _____ (I would say), I put it to you once more that; or, Would it not be fair to say that, given your previous statements. Or I might present him with certain indisputable facts, with all imaginable supporting evidence, and invite him to explain or dispute these facts, if he could. Or sometimes I would pose quite simple questions about, for example, the weather. How would you describe the weather today? Overcast? Blustery? Threatening? Unsettled? All simple, easy, leading questions. Or I might try to explore his opinion on the influence of sunny days as against overcast days in terms of their relative effect on mood, psychology, even decision-making in certain instances. Notwithstanding, he certainly seemed, whatever the current state of the weather, to have a favourite view from the window - I could tell due to the very slight lean angle of his upper body, which indicated to me that he was looking towards the stark mountain range in the distance.

Out of frustration I began - and even then only now and again - to make animal noises - the howling of a coyote, the screeching of birds in the canopy, the constant background calls of nocturnal insects and frogs in a rainforest at night, just to try to get some suggestion of a response, on the basis that any hint of a response was better than none. And though I thought at times I detected a slight flicker of the eyeballs at, for example, my impression of a macaque emitting warning calls from the upper branches on spotting a leopard prowling the jungle floor below, it was never enough to produce any definitive reaction.

And sometimes as I watched him gaze through the window towards the mountains, unspeaking, I would wonder what he was thinking about, if anything. However, I generally forbore to ask - it seemed far too personal, too intrusive a line of questioning, given everything that had gone before.

The Old Man

There was once this old man with a walker who always looked steadily at me with a look of dislike and utter contempt, as if he knew all my dirty little secrets. I never knew why. He'd be trundling at zero mph down the corridor, then abruptly turn and give me that look. I took to taking elaborate precautions in an attempt to avoid unexpected encounters. Once I was walking up to the building, comprised of multiple flats on three levels, and there he was, staring down at me in a threatening manner from a communal lounge on the first floor. I always tried to keep my composure, but to then enter the building, be walking along a corridor and see ten yards ahead his face slowly appear around a corner, sticking out at a strange angle, as if two people were holding his legs and lifting him into that position, was unpleasant and disconcerting in equal measure. I quickly retreated and found a different route to my flat. And why such animosity? What did I ever do to him, apart from rap on his door smartly with my pool cue whenever I happened to be passing. And occasionally push abusive notes through his letterbox in the early hours, for him to find and read in the morning. The whole affair was inexplicable. But Time found the solution, as it always does, and I unfortunately died soon after our final confrontation. Which put a hard stop to the matter.

Miriam

Only that very day had I met Miriam. And only that one day would I ever spend with her, as I never saw or heard of her again, despite asking for her number - as a friend, nothing more. I had no illusions.

'Why don't you come onto the aeroplane to say goodbye?'

'Is that allowed?'

'I'm sure it'll be fine if no-one notices.'

And somehow it was.

We'd spent the day together in an obscure corner of the Yorkshire Dales looking for a derelict Elizabethan farmhouse that in some unspecified way I knew to be in the area somewhere, though unclear as to its exact location. And Miriam was somehow beside me that day, a gentle, calm and calming presence, imbuing everything we encountered with meaning and immediacy. I experienced a feeling of wonder that day as never before or since, as if every tree and every stone, even every last blade of grass, had a meaning and clarity it had never possessed before and would never possess again. As if every last thing we encountered that day could never have been anything other than exactly how and where and what it was, and all presenting in the most startling limpidity. And everything flowed from Miriam in some mysterious way beyond all understanding, as if everything, regardless of its beauty and splendour, only existed because of her.

Walking together up a rough grassy lane between tumbledown stone walls, looking for a way that would lead to the derelict farmhouse, I surveyed a lane leading steeply to a scatter of farm buildings above us, but couldn't see there what we sought. Another lane leading off and up, and again no sign of the farmhouse. The lane we currently pursued now broadened out, with ahead of us a break where a stone wall had collapsed in a scatter of stones, allowing access to yet another lane leading up.

And at this point we were met with a large herd of sheep that emerged directly in front of us, all bleating loudly in a heady cacophony and appearing uncharacteristically aggressive. Several viewed us with what looked like serious intent in their dull eyes, as if about to charge, and at this I experienced a moment of high anxiety, though Miriam appeared entirely unconcerned, calm and composed as ever. And then, as they began running wildly, scattering in all directions, with Miriam and I caught in the maelstrom, something quite wonderful occurred. One after another the larger and more threatening of the sheep executed an abrupt backward somersault, landing on their backs and thereafter staying motionless as if stunned. Sheep being imitative animals and easily led (at least that was my first surmise), they all began flipping onto their backs such that the lane was filled with the bizarre sight of a legion of hooves all pointing to the sky.

Just as we reached the break in the wall, from behind us and seemingly from nowhere came a bunch of young people on bicycles all cycling pell-mell, who then launched themselves over us so that all we saw were the shadows of the riders on their bikes as they passed above us and then disappeared from sight. We clambered over the fallen stones, still wondering about the strange behaviour of the sheep, to be met with a tall farmgirl of perhaps eighteen or nineteen dressed in black leggings, sturdy boots and sweat-stained t-shirt. She was a magnificent specimen, clearly raised on hard physical labour, her thighs strong and supple, her upper body exuding strength. Her face was long and pale, her features strong, her shoulder length straw-blonde hair tied back in a neat ponytail. All her physical characteristics suggested a direct Scandinavian lineage.

Upon inquiry regarding the curious behaviour of the sheep she explained in understated tones that it was due to a local phenomenon known as the circular loopstone, a strong naturally occurring magnetic force found in local rock formations that occasionally interfered with the brain function of sheep. She said it was sheer coincidence that we had seen this happen before our eyes, as it was in fact quite a rare occurrence. We asked her about her work, which consisted of freelancing on local farms, and of course she knew of the Elizabethan farmhouse, and was able to give us precise directions. We thanked her, set off up the hill and quickly found it.

I'd first been attracted to the building after coming across photos in an old travel guide to the area. It was immediately clear as it came into view that it had deteriorated badly since the photos were taken back in the late 1930s. The illustrations had shown an intact though derelict stone building, compact and unpretentious, with attached barn, a roof of large stone slabs, squat chimney, and a line of rectangular windows divided into lights by stone mullions. Neglect and lack of habitation and maintenance had left the building vulnerable to years of ice and frost and strong winds off the high moor, and once a breach in the roof had been established deterioration had doubtless been swift. We found the roof entirely collapsed inwards, the porch gone, the attractive windows filled in with building material, and the tops of the walls disintegrating. In short, the farmhouse was now just a ruin.

I was affected deeply by the sight of such heedless devastation. I sat down on a grassy bank just by the ruin and covered my face with my hands, trying unsuccessfully to hide my emotions. Miriam sat down alongside me, comforting me with softly spoken, well-chosen words of consolation, though her presence alone was consolation enough.

And so to our final goodbyes, overshadowed somewhat by my anxiety that the door would be closed before I had a chance to exit the aeroplane, with all the complications that would inevitably entail. As we embarked on our final valedictions I happened to catch a brief glimpse of a document Miriam was holding, which gave her name as something quite different from what I had naturally supposed was her given name. She explained that she had never been happy with her name, and had therefore chosen to call herself Miriam, attracted by how it sounded, and by the story of 'Miriam the Prophetess' (sister of Moses and Aaron) in the Book of Exodus, and the many representations of her in art, particularly that by Anselm Feuerbach (in fact a model by the name of Anna Risi). Completely won over by this explanation - though needless to say none was strictly necessary - I replied that, yes, of course, in an ideal world one's name should be a free choice.

And so we parted. And since then my life has been a hollow shell, devoid of meaning. An empty husk. A void.

Miriam. Wonderful, unforgettable, peerless Miriam, you have left me bereft.

The Search for Meaning

I decided to test the theory that there is meaning and synchronicity in the universe, an interrelation of psyche and matter, using my dog as test subject. First I painted with edible colouring 11:11 on his bone, just to see if it made any difference. It didn't. Then I painted 11:11 on his food bowl, just to see if that made any difference. It didn't - he took a dump with the same relentless regularity as before. So I tried a different tack. I buried his bowl in the garden and tried hard to forget where I'd buried it. Then I took a ride on the subway in the hope and expectation that someone would have left behind a dog's bowl of the exact same type as the one I'd just buried, and that this bowl would have 11:11 painted on the side of it. Needless to say, no bowl was forthcoming. I returned home, dug up the buried bowl, cleaned it and fed the dog, who by this time was beside himself with hunger. I decided on a fresh approach. I wanted to find out if the faculties of my dog's psyche were indeed confined to space and time, or whether the dog had dreams and visions of the future amounting to premonitions; in other words, whether there was indeed a mystical correspondence between the inner realm of the psyche, and the external world in a dance of cosmic reflection. I recognised at once that this would present a difficult problem in terms of establishing a reliable investigative tool. So I decided instead to rely entirely on my own imagination and inability to think logically, in any meaningful sense of the term, and therefore to make it all up as I went along. So I positioned my armchair such as to allow an unfettered view of my dog as he lay in his bed, and so as to ensure that I stayed alert at all times I assembled a ready supply of snacks and alcoholic drinks within easy reaching distance. And as I watched the dog blissfully sleeping, twitching and moving its jaws in a repetitive action that I could clearly interpret as chewing on a bone, I was suddenly struck by the sight of a half-chewed bone almost but not quite hidden by the dog's tail, and was immediately overwhelmed by this incontrovertible evidence of synchronicity. That is until I remembered that I'd given the dog the bone earlier in the day, and it had been there on his bed all along. Disappointed, I turned my chair instead towards the TV, and ate and drank until I passed out.

To My Daughter

Dear Sarah,

Three years ago you sent me an email saying goodbye, and as you know I haven't seen or spoken to you since then. You had a lot to say in this email, but the gist of it was that I'd been literally the worst mother in the world. That you hated my political views and opinions, that you were sick of having to tiptoe around my moods - which is odd, as my recollection is that you were always the one with the difficult moods, certainly as a teen - that you were sick of being lied to and gaslighted, tired of being guilt-tripped over everything that you supposedly had or hadn't done, and that you couldn't tolerate my narcissism any longer, my complete lack of self-awareness, my self-absorption, where every single thing, whether it was your birthdays, your relationships, even your graduation, somehow invariably became all about me. In short, I had ruined your life. And so you had decided it would be better if I were no longer a part of it.

All of this came without any warning whatsoever. It was as if you'd had a road to Damascus revelation that I was the most hateful person in the world, someone who had to be unceremoniously cut out of your life, excised like a tumor for the sake of your mental health and so that you could heal and regain some peace of mind. Which again is odd, as you never had any mental health problems, so far as I'm aware. The overall message was that you needed space, and didn't want any communication or contact between us for the time being.

So that was the bombshell that hit me out of nowhere, took the ground from under my feet and sent me into freefall. I was too shocked on initial reading to do anything but collapse on the sofa. I literally could do nothing for the rest of that day, going over and over and over your message such that it quickly became impressed or ingrained into my brain like deep scratch marks on paint. My entire life had been upended and everything I had done for you throughout your childhood and over the course of your adult life, a period of almost thirty years, had been erased, its worth reduced to nothing in one lengthy email setting out in detail all my shortcomings in cold, hard, emotionless language that left no room for discussion, mediation, or second chances. The tears, endless, wracking floods of tears as the reality sank in that my only daughter had disowned me came soon enough and continued almost unrelentingly for the first few weeks.

Once I was over that initial period of extreme shock, I started frantically reviewing in my mind every interaction between us that I could recall in which the seeds of estrangement might have been sown. And of course, when I could bear to confront the past without gloss or filter, I came across a few things - not many - that I deeply regret. Times I didn't do something I could have done, and other times I did something I bitterly wish I hadn't. But only a few things really stand out over that thirty year period. Every parent, if they're honest with themselves, has a similar story to tell. After all, you're on display to your child 24/7. Every day of their life they see your every fault, annoying habit, quirk and foible in pitiless close-up. There's no hiding place. Probably every child goes through a period of embarrassment at their parents' failings, of feeling short-changed at discovering their feet of clay, and for some a phase of hating and despising. But then as they reach adulthood and face the challenges of adult life, many - probably most - learn to forgive. If they have children themselves they soon learn that being a parent is like being on a tightrope while simultaneously being under a microscope. So most learn eventually to forgive, or at least find some measure of compromise within themselves that allows them to keep their parent or parents in their lives. And of course some don't.

After giving myself a week to absorb the implications of your letter, I wrote you an equally long email in reply. Telling you, if you recall, that I loved you no matter what, but that our memories of past events necessarily differ, and that surely even if we have political differences and different ways of looking at society, can we not amicably agree to disagree? And that I didn't really understand what you were meaning about gaslighting (I had to google the term just to learn what it meant) and guilt-tripping, because as I say people will always have conflicting recollections of things that happened ten, fifteen, twenty years ago (or even last week or yesterday), which is why eyewitness testimony in court has to be treated with extreme caution. And hadn't I always encouraged you to do the things you wanted to do, and to strive for your goals, whatever they might be?

Anyway, I wrote, the bottom line was that I loved you, had done my best as a mom, and no parent was perfect - and so on along these lines, expressing contrition, if that's what you needed to hear, though I wasn't sure what I was supposed to be contrite about. After several days of anxious waiting I at last received a reply, telling me that I was still not listening, that this was exactly what you'd been talking about, that I hadn't respected your request to give you space. And that this time it was final, and please not to contact you again. I expect you remember all of this. Or maybe you remember it all differently.

I hadn't said anything to family before this, perhaps because it seemed like confessing to the ultimate failure. But after this latest blow I finally told your aunt. Her reaction was like mine, utter disbelief, then indignation and anger on my behalf, when she knew what I'd been through in the early years of your childhood, the horror period of the divorce from your dad, managing to keep a roof over our heads and food on the table, providing unconditional love plus all kinds of opportunities for you growing up, and all as a one-parent family. Then university, helping you to buy a car, giving you the deposit to rent a flat. And the more we talked, and it was a relief and release to share what had happened, the more angry Carolyn became. So she texted you - I think she might have been less than diplomatic - and you immediately blocked her. You'd always been on good terms, so it was quite upsetting for your aunt. Carolyn told other family members and family friends, some of whom reached out to me, and some of whom texted or emailed you, without my knowledge or permission, and which I'm sure was counterproductive.

So months passed, and my birthday came and went unacknowledged, which was hard to take and again put me in a tailspin for a while, amid more desolate days and evenings and nights filled with tears and despair. And when your birthday came around I sent you a loving message with birthday wishes telling you how much I missed you and loved you and hoped you were doing well. Zero response. And then gradually as time passed and I was able to gain some kind of perspective on what had happened, I began to join up the dots on the timing of that fateful email. We've always disagreed on religion and politics ever since you were in your teens. When you were thirteen you suddenly stopped coming to church, refusing outright to have anything to do with it, saying there was no God, and that it was all superstitious nonsense. And as church and trying to live a Christian life is extremely important to me, and I love and worship Jesus with all my heart, I found this deeply hurtful.

Following your rejection of Christianity, you went through a short-lived Goth phase, followed by a militant feminist phase, then a vegan phase - all these overlapping somewhat. And then, presumably thinking you hadn't provoked me sufficiently by this time, a full-on Communist phase, complete with a copy of *Das Kapital* on your bedside table (did you ever read it?), and posters of Lenin and Che Guevara on the walls of your bedroom. All of which I thought fairly standard stuff for an intelligent girl of your age, if a little predictable, not to say passé, and assumed that you would quickly grow out of it. Though some of the looks I caught you giving me around this period were pretty lethal, ranging from mild dislike to deep loathing. But like I say, many teens can't stand their parents at this stage of their lives, and for most it is just a phase.

I'd received that first, devastating email in March of 2021. Only later, as I say, did I understand the significance of the timing. You'd come home for Christmas in the wake of the presidential election, so inevitably the conversation, if you can call it that - more a series of hate-filled diatribes directed against me and the whole MAGA movement - centred around the issue of a stolen election amid systemic voter fraud. I refused to refer to Biden as the president, as I didn't regard his election as legitimate, and any mention of President Trump resulted in predictable outbursts of hatred from you. And then came Jan 6 and the protest at the Capitol, conducted peacefully enough for the most part, apart from a few Antifa provocateurs stirring up trouble and inciting violence. We watched it all unfolding on TV, if you remember, both of us too shocked by what we were seeing to say much.

The next day you left after a particularly unhappy, acrimonious Christmas. And though I didn't know it at the time, that would be the last time I would ever see you. It took a couple of months of, I like to think, agonising over your decision, or maybe it was just building up your courage, before you sent the email cutting off all contact. And in hindsight - I don't know if you agree - Jan 6 and its aftermath seem clearly to be the catalyst for the estrangement that followed.

And if the topic of a stolen election and voter fraud weren't enough to inflame your emotions, there were always the longstanding contentious issues of immigration and abortion. Here in Florida we've been overrun by illegal immigrants, but so much as a mention of this entirely reasonable concern and you would immediately accuse me of being a Nazi who'd like nothing more than to see all immigrants rounded up and put in a concentration camp. And as for abortion, I've always believed that human life is sacred, that life begins at conception, and that abortion in normal circumstances is immoral, against the will of God, and in fact murder of an innocent. But any suggestion of views along these lines was to invite a tsunami of hostility and soundbite invective: stop the war on women, hands off women's bodies, abortion is a human right, women's rights are human rights, my body, my choice and so on and so on. Whereas my concern was more with the body of the little proto-human, dependent and defenceless, inside the mother's womb. Had we still been in contact, the overturning of Roe v Wade would doubtless have unleashed a fresh firestorm of vitriol on the subject from you. In fact I happen know that it did, though not directed specifically at me.

Your aunt told me one day she'd come across your YouTube channel, which I had no idea even existed. Just to be able to see you again and hear your voice was both wonderful and extremely emotional. Maybe once a week, as if to catch up with you, I'd watch your latest video, often with tears streaming down my face. And it was via this channel that I received a shock almost as overwhelming as that first email. From watching your channel I gathered that the focus was on mental health, with some political comment and occasional diversions into film and book reviews. Later videos, hideously enough from my standpoint, discussed estrangement from parents from a firsthand perspective, though it was a long time before I could face watching those.

But a year or so on, having given up on ever seeing you again, and with your YouTube channel my only remaining connection to you, there came, as I say, the first hints of the second calamitous shock. I'd noticed that you had begun to dress in a masculine way and had cut your hair very short, but hadn't thought too much about it. In fact I thought it looked very becoming, and suited you. That was until you announced your intention of transitioning to a male, telling your audience that you would henceforth identify as male, and asking everyone watching and commenting on the channel to use male pronouns when referring to you.

While I knew that you were sympathetic to the LGBT community, it would never have crossed my mind in a million years that you would follow this path. It didn't seem real at first, more like playacting or a cry for attention. But then you started telling your viewers, who without exception were hugely supportive, of your intention to have surgery. So you outlined the process of transitioning, starting with a course of testosterone. But when you began to describe the surgery, first a double mastectomy, then removal of all the organs that make you a female, and then onto so-called 'bottom surgery' (phalloplasty), I couldn't bear to watch or listen any further, and in fact gave up watching the channel for the best part of a year. All I could think was, No, no, no, you'll ruin your body forever, you'll regret it for the rest of your life. Call yourself a man if you like, make people call you he and him and his, but don't mutilate your body, because if you do there's no going back.

A year or so later I managed to steel myself to take another look at your channel, only to be confronted by this bearded dude with a deep voice called Sam. After a moment's incomprehension I realised that this meant a final goodbye to my beautiful daughter. And now, a year and a half further on, the idea of you as a man is more or less normalized in my mind, as much as it ever can be.

So finally, as my last word, I just want to tell you that I still love you so much, Sarah. Every day I miss your face and your voice and your laughter. More than anything I simply miss you being around, and being around you. But I respect your decision to pursue an independent life, and I'm sorry I couldn't live up to your expectations as a mother. I know that you will probably never read this, but I'll leave it among my effects, my will and so on, to be found and read one day, or not. And now I shall close and say my final goodbye to you.

Wishing you all the joy and happiness in the world,

Mom

The Lodge House

But what if there was no lodge house? Merely great rusting iron gates, paint flaking, left ajar. I look for the foundations of the vanished lodge and see only faint traces, which could be anything. The Hall is long gone, demolished in the fifties as so many great houses were, victims of the inheritance tax. And there appear to be no authenticated photos of the lodge house, understandable given that everyone's interest and attention in its halcyon days would have been on the main house and all the ongoing activities in and around it.

A local artist was reputed to have made a number of sketches of the Hall, which could possibly have included the lodge - if indeed it ever existed - though she was more renowned for her striking depictions of industrial scenes within the town - the mills and factories, workers making their way to and from their places of employment. This was back in the thirties, and I wasn't even sure if the artist was still alive. If she was, then she would have to be very aged, with possibly a poor recollection of what she had painted, and when, at least in any detail. Still, I thought it worth a visit, speculative at best, to her bungalow in extensive grounds on the edge of town, which I knew to contain her studio.

Naturally I'd heard the persistent dark rumours, that as a result of professional disappointment she'd become dangerously eccentric, and had taken to locking her long-suffering husband, who before his retirement had been some kind of an official in India, in the garage for long periods of time. Of course I discounted these rumours as fantastical, the kind of nonsense that spreads like bindweed where there exist no clear and indisputable facts to refute such scurrilous tales. And moreover this artist had been practically a recluse for the past ten years or more, enough in itself to feed the rumour mill.

Yet when I pulled into the side of the lane, got out of the car and went up to the gates of the artist's property, I found them chained, and the chain itself rusty with disuse, which for some reason struck me as particularly ominous. And there just off the drive to the left and at the far end was the garage. Now, with the physical layout in front of me, and the rumours to the forefront of my mind, it was easy for imagination to run riot, and see the artist frogmarching her husband from the house, one arm bent up behind his back, pleading impotently. This once acclaimed artist, tall, thin, angular, unmoved, relentlessly, perhaps even psychotically determined, opens the garage door, pushes her husband inside and slams the door shut, shooting the bolt, and additionally securing the door with a shiny new padlock, bought especially for the purpose.

But even these precautions may not have been enough to hold the artist's husband, if certain fresh rumours are to be believed. That over many months and years he had constructed a labyrinth of tunnels under not just the house, but the entire property, which might well have included the garage. The key question, if such rumours could be believed, was whether the artist was aware of this activity. To my mind it beggars belief that she would not be. But still it's an open question as to whether she knew the extent of the excavations. I think it quite possible that yes, of course she was well aware of her husband's activities, and may even have welcomed them as relieving her of his presence, which for a creative spirit may have had a dulling, deadening effect. But that such activities extended as far as the garage is another matter, and something she may well not have considered possible. And if she did indeed fail to factor in this possibility in her efforts to more or less permanently secure and restrain her husband, then shutting him in the garage may well not have achieved the desired objective. And even now he may be somewhere below the house and grounds, prowling the dark and dusty maze-like network of corridors he had himself created.

Perfidy

I was about to say I'm disappointed, but in fact disappointment implies expectations, and I have learnt to have none. However, you made certain promises, certain explicit commitments to me personally, which I accepted in good faith, and which you have failed entirely to fulfil. I don't want here and now to go into the sordid details of this - I could almost say betrayal, but let us say failure, or its effect upon me, my family and even my reputation. Suffice it to say that broken promises, lies and bad faith are like cancer spots on the liver, they are a canker that spreads until the entire body is riddled and corrupt. Your derelictions of faith redound to your dishonour and almost inevitable long-term degradation, much more than to any disadvantage they may have brought to me. Oh by all means say whatever you have to say - of course you have the right of rebuttal - if you think that anything useful *can* be said in defence of your outrageous behaviour.

You would do well to drop that rather challenging tone, as if you were addressing an obstreperous housemaid. Such tactics will gain you nothing, and merely underline your obstinacy and intransigence, which together with an ill-advised arrogance and lack of moral centre are among your least attractive qualities. Of course now I wonder that I was taken in so readily. The letters of recommendation, the references from esteemed public figures, the projections of profit, the guarantees of security, all designed to secure investment in this phantom venture - and all false, all illusory, all in fact directed towards a single goal, that of lining your own pockets. That I *was* taken in by all the completely unfounded bona fides - and, I confess, the superficial charm, which you lavished generously on all my family as we welcomed you into our hearth and home - does, I admit, little credit to my powers of perception and good judgement. Hence the fact that as this affair inevitably becomes common knowledge the damage to my reputation will be considerable. I really do not see what more you can have to say on this matter, or what you can possibly put forward in your defence.

So, you inquire, in that ridiculously high-handed manner, and with a mocking smirk on your face, what steps I intend to take. As if you have any control now over your destiny, and as if your reputation, such as it ever was, is not now forever destroyed. I have to tell you, and not with any pleasure or desire for retribution, that you are ruined beyond recall, at least so far as any kind of public life is concerned. Have no doubt on that score. And let that fact sink in and wipe that smirk off your face, if anything can. At the same time I hope that there may one day be some measure of private contrition, of acceptance of responsibility for your actions and, possibly, at some distant point in the future, redemption. As for my immediate steps, informing the police will be first among them.

You expect me to believe this most heinous of lies! How dare you! How dare you besmirch my daughter's good name with this most vile implication. If I were not a man of peace, I would without hesitation give you a sound beating this very moment. I cannot begin to express the horror and disgust I feel at both your shameless perfidy, and your odious attempt to involve my daughter. That you successfully ingratiated yourself with my family is something I acknowledge, and deeply regret. That it went any further than that, and with my daughter…No, you may not bring her into this room, that her ears may be polluted…Maria! My daughter, tell me this is not true. Tell me you haven't…involved yourself with this man. Tell me it isn't true. Tell me that this creature, with all he has done to us, and against us, has not visited upon our family this final and greatest indignity. Tell me it is not so…

Then We'll be Done

I was walking down the prom to the tram stop, and I couldn't stop wondering if I'd cleaned under Mrs Chadwick's sofa. Of course, it's not the end of the world if I haven't. But I like to do a proper job, and if you miss it once the dust starts to accumulate. Sofas are the worst thing because you can't move them, you have to get down on your hands and knees even to get the hoover under. And then all the stuff you find underneath. You have to have a clear-out before the hoover, or you just end up blocking the machine, and then it's a right faff taking it apart and freeing it up. Bits of toys, marbles, sweet wrappers, you name it, you find all sorts under sofas. And then all that bending gets my back these days. In fact just going round with the hoover has been giving me a bit of backache lately. Probably just a passing phase.

Mrs Chadwick has her grandkids come round once a fortnight on the Sunday. She shows me photos after I've made her a cup of tea, and right little terrors they look, two boys, eight and six, and apparently when they come round it's like a whirlwind's hit the place. She's a drawer with toys in it for the kiddies, cars, a wooden train set, jigsaws, lego and the like, so they go straight for that to start with, then ten minutes later there's toys everywhere and they're arguing over them, then into all the cupboards, then taking all the ornaments off the shelves, shouting and squabbling, wrestling, in and out of the house, bringing in muck from the garden on their shoes, demanding something to eat and drink. She says, don't get me wrong, I love seeing them, but an hour or so once a fortnight's about enough, even though her daughter's there, and of course it's nice to have a chat, as much as you can with all the noise and disruption. And then it takes an age to get the place straight again, and after she needs a nice quiet cup of tea and a lie down. Says she can't imagine what it's like having them around full-time, she'd be pulling her hair out, though no doubt she'd have managed if she was younger. Anyway after chatting with Mrs Chadwick for a bit I set to and get the place straight, then nip out for some shopping she needs. Last thing on a visit I'll have a go round with the hoover and make sure there's nothing lurking under the sofa, if I don't forget, that is (I think I must have been distracted by the back pain). And then we'll be done.

Marriage just never happened for me for some reason. Not for want of suitors - well one or two, at least, but it never went anywhere. I sometimes think, if I'd had a daughter I might have had grandkids by now. They'd have come round to visit, with their bonny round faces, and all their endless chatter and noise, and disturbing everything and what have you, and…I wouldn't have minded a bit. It would have been a small price to pay. But anyway it wasn't to be. So once I've finished for the day and I'm in and I've had my tea…there's just me.

A lot of my clients are smokers, but I'm used to it after all this time. Still, I shove everything in the washer when I get back to get rid of the smell. Mr Beasley's the worst. Nice enough man, but smokes like a chimney. You go in and it's like a thick fog, and he's in his armchair with the telly on, and the ashtrays are overflowing, and he's got his whisky and his vodka and bottles of coke and whatnot to hand. So first thing I do is open all the windows. I felt apologetic the first time, as if I was making a point, but he apologised to me, said he doesn't notice how bad it gets and to go right ahead and get some fresh air into the place. I just don't know how he can live like that. Of course I don't think he will be living like that much longer. He's got emphysema, constantly coughing, his breathing's never clear, you can hear him from the kitchen, but he refuses to give it up, says it's his one pleasure. Used to be a bus driver, said his last route before he retired was the no.7 and no.14 from Talbot Road bus station through to Fleetwood. Not a route I know, so I said I don't think I'll ever have been on the bus when you were the driver. But he used to do other routes before that, so I suppose it's possible. Anyway after a nice little chat and making him a cup of tea I set to and do the bedding and get a load in the washer, then do the washing up and have a general tidy up and clean through the house. It's a nice terraced house at the back of Gynn Square, so I usually take the tram down. There's upstairs and downstairs so there's a fair bit of work to do, and I was really feeling it today for some reason, and after vacuuming the place up and down my back was killing me, and I was thinking I can't go on like this, I'm going to have to go and see the doctor. Which is a real nuisance as I've got commitments right through the week, and anyway it's near impossible to see a doctor these days. But I'm going to have to do something as I can't go on like this. Anyway after I was done I popped out for some cigarettes - he practically buys them in bulk - then made Mr Beasley a cup of tea and asked him if he wanted the windows open or shut before I go. He said, would you mind closing them. It's difficult for him to get around now, even from one room to another. His bedroom's in what would have been the drawing room as there's no way for him to get upstairs, so they've put a small ensuite bathroom in, and a carer comes a couple of times a week to help give him a clean-up. So last thing I'll close the windows, and Mr Beasley'll always thank me several times and smile and wave as I'm walking out - like I say, a nice man, a gentleman. And then we'll be done.

I live in Bispham, which is a smallish village just north of Blackpool proper, and that's where most of my clients are. Not all, I've a couple up in town like Mr Beasley, or going the other way Mrs Chadwick. I sometimes have my dinner at a café, just down from the front. Not every day, that would add up, just once a week as a little treat. In fact where I live is just a bit further down Red Bank Road from the café, but on the other side, a nice little flat above the shops. It does for me quite nicely, it's only small, easy enough to heat. So if my next client's in

Bispham I'll usually go home for my dinner, but it's nice once in a while to go to the café. Makes a change, and it's company even though I don't usually see anyone I know, it's mainly tourists through the season. Or I might take some sandwiches and a flask if it's a nice day and sit on a bench on the prom and look out at the sea and pretend I'm a tourist on my holidays. But then it's back down to earth and back to work.

The doctor says I need to go to the hospital for further tests as a matter of some priority. Which is not really what you want to hear, so that got me thinking. But he didn't give much away. Said he didn't like the colour of my eyes, and that coupled with the back pain was suggestive, but he didn't say of what. So it's more faffing about when I really haven't got the time. But he was emphatic that I attend, and said he thought it would be quite a quick appointment, and I didn't much like the sound of that either. I'd far rather he'd said it was just routine and there was no particular hurry. I wish they'd just trust people with the facts. I'd rather know what was going on than be left in the dark. And there may be nothing in it anyway, and then it's all fuss and worry for nothing. Doesn't make sense to me, but you can't argue with doctors. You'd probably get struck off or whatever it is if you made a fuss.

Mrs Holdsworth lives up from Red Bank Road, quite a hill, and today I was puffing and blowing, which is not like me at all, and to be honest that is a bit of a worry. A nice, tidy little semi, neat as a pin inside, the garden just as neat - I think she gets a man in. Mrs Holdsworth is a very quiet, timid sort of woman, friendly enough, a spinster, though you're probably not allowed to use that word these days. And worst thing is I'm technically in the same boat, though I don't think of myself like that. Not that I'm interested anymore, that's all past. She's always wearing a pinafore over when I go round, off-white with a roses pattern on it, reds and yellows, as if she's just ready to set to, and to be honest there's not a whole lot for me to do as a rule. I change the bedding and put a wash on, then do the bathroom, though I'm pretty sure she's been round it before I come. There's a mobile shop comes round once a week, but if there's anything she needs I'll pop down to the shops, as it's a bit of a trek down and especially up again. When I take a break for a cup of tea she insists on making it herself in a teapot, with a pretty little cup and saucer from a set, and a plate with fancy cakes to choose from. I'm pretty sure I'm there mainly as a familiar face and someone to chat to for half an hour, more sometimes. And what you can't help noticing as we sit and chat about this and that - she says she can often hear the kiddies playing in the garden next door, and sometimes they'll call round and ask if there's anything they can do for her, nice children, a girl and a boy, so well-behaved, a rarity these days - anyway you can't help noticing the photos everywhere, on the mantelpiece, on an occasional table, on the sideboard, all of the same man at different ages. You'd naturally think it was her husband, but turns out it's her brother. They lived together in the house for fifty-odd years, him going out to work, her keeping house and ready with the evening meal when he got back, for all the world like a married couple. That's until he died two years ago, and now she lives there with just a cat for company, a great fat fluffy thing that never moves and leaves hairs everywhere, at least I've never seen it move, it just sleeps in a cat bed next to the fireplace all day long. My back was playing up again today, so I had to cry off for once, but as a rule last thing I'll go round with the hoover, though like I say the place is practically spotless. And I'll bring the washing in if it's a warm day and it's dried, and put it away, else put it on a drier inside. And then we'll be done.

Haven't heard anything from the hospital yet, so I was back at Mrs Chadwick's today. It was meant to be their retirement dream, Mrs Chadwick and her late husband, a nice bungalow just off the prom towards Cleveleys. She showed me photos and to be honest he never looked well, sallow skin and puffy face, prime candidate for a coronary by the look of him. She didn't say if that's what happened, but that's what it looked like to me. Six months they had together in the bungalow, then he was gone. Funny how often that happens, people retire after working all their lives, find themselves at a complete loss when they stop, then next thing you know they've popped off. I'm lucky, I'm kept occupied, a full roster of clients. And it's not a bad life, when you come right down to it, and if I do get tired sometimes that's normal at my time of life. And anyway what's the alternative, sitting at home doing nothing all day? That's not for me, I'm too used to being busy. I'm not even sure I could take that kind of life for long, I'd probably end up like the rest. Anyway I just need to go once round with the hoover, make sure I check under the sofa this time, and make Mrs Chadwick a nice cup of tea before I go.

So the consultant said, 'How do you want to handle this?' And I was thinking at the time, that's a strange thing to say, how does anyone handle it. As best they can is the best anyone can do. But he meant do you want to go into a hospice at some point, or get end of life care at home. Well that was spelling it out right enough. Not that I had to make the decision there and then. Anyway I'd already decided I'll stick it out in my own place till the end, as best I can. That's always been my motto, just do as best you can. That's how I've always been, making the most of things, even when it's not much. Sounds bitter saying it like that, but I'm not. So I'll see it through at home. I don't want any help or fuss. I don't want carers calling in at all hours. I'll see to myself, somehow, as I've always done. So long as I've got painkillers towards the end I should be right. There's no sense in fussing. What's that old saying - What can't be cured must be endured. Well they can't cure this one, it's got a ninety-five percent fatality rate. But it is what it is. Anyway I've saved up a bit over the years, so I can stop working anytime. I can't carry on anyway, I haven't the energy. So I can have a nice little rest, a quiet time. I could take the tram down to Fleetwood now and then, get some fish and chips. Or watch the telly all day if I want to, with nothing to do. And I'll get everything straight - I don't want any loose ends. I'll get the flat tidy and all the paperwork and arrangements in place. Make sure everything's taken care of. And then we'll be done.

Jackwagon Blues

I can't tell you how sick I am of other people, and everything - in that order. Okay, I will then. Thing is, I've done the nice. I shouldn't have to keep on doing it indefinitely. But they never take a hint, never just keep silent, respectfully look the other way and hold their flapping tongues. Always, always the assumption, the mistaken, preposterous assumption, that I would want to speak to them, would want to hear what they have to say, drink in their ignorance, be sickened by their opinions, bored to distraction by their everlasting stories of childhood, jobs, spouses, children, holidays etc. etc. as every last puerile detail in their empty heads comes rattling out. And each encounter reduces me in every way by just that little bit, incrementally eroding me, drip by tedious drip. And like I say, I've made the nice, been pleasant, smiled, listened, stood there wishing that either the world would end, or I, or they, would drop dead on the spot.

And still it goes on, eroding, wearing down, wearing away. While they assume - and this is the funny part, the awful part that fills me with homicidal rage when I'm not shrieking with hostile internal laughter as I walk away - they assume that I would want to see them and listen to their endless banalities. Part of the problem is getting older, you get battle fatigue. Or as I call it, human fatigue. You just can't bear the presence any longer of these jackanapes, these soul-crushing jackwagons.

The Melancholy of the Hour

A late afternoon turning to dusk in that liminal space between light and dark, sound and silence, being and non-being. The time when all the phantoms, ghosts and demons come out to play, make trouble and torment. Not that I really believe in such things.

The leaves have fallen and been trodden into a slippery mush. It's colder, but not yet freezing. The streets are deserted, and the shadows are growing longer, less distinct. Chilled, I begin the short walk home.

Home. What images that word conjures of warmth, companionship, comfort, security, cosy familiarity and familial chat around the fireside. Instead, I begin the short walk home to my social housing flat, a frigid, friendless place, but of course better than living on the streets.

Lately I've begun to think more often about the chance of falling and lying undisturbed, undiscovered, for days, weeks, maybe months. I've been thinking some kind of alarm system I can carry around with me might be an idea. But why would I want to be found? To continue with this pale apology for life?

There's a small amount of shopping to be done. A few remembered items which will save me having to go out again later. I buy these things - a box of tissues, a pint of milk, a can of soup and a bread roll for my tea, to be followed by tinned peaches for pudding - and return 'home'.

I turn the electric heater in the living room on one bar to take the hard edge off the chill. Then get myself a cup of tea and digestive biscuit and take them through. Cover my lower half with a blanket and switch on the telly.

And that's pretty much me done for the day. Highlights? Countdown, Deal or No Deal, The Chase. I watch these religiously every day, and never miss the news at 6 o'clock, though to be honest it's got little or nothing to do with me. Later on there's Inspector Frost or Midsomer Murders.

And as I say that's me done for the day. Make a bottle last thing and pop it in the bed to warm it up before I get in. And then the best part of my existence. Oblivion.

What Is Is

So there it is. There you have it. That is the answer, and the only possible answer, to the question that demanded no answer. Or in the words of a great philosopher, 'I expect nothing, and am never disappointed.' Or to put it another way, if it had been possible to do things another way, I would have done them another way. If there had been a viable alternative, I would have taken that alternative. But there wasn't. In the end, everything took the course it did, because that was the course it took. And that's pretty much the way things are. What is is.

Printed in Great Britain
by Amazon